Asher's Story

A BLACKSTONE ACADEMY NOVELLA

Elizabeth Dear

Copyright © 2022 by Elizabeth Dear Publishing LLC

Editing by Hot Tree Editing

Cover by Cherie Foxley

Formatting by Elizabeth Dear and Stephanie Osu, PA

All Rights Reserved.

No Part of this book may be reproduced in any form or by any electronic or mechanical means, including information storage and retrieval systems, without written permission from the author, except for brief quotations in a book review.

This one's for Megan, a true friend who couldn't leave for vacation without her paperback of Knox and had to let herself into my house like a sneaky thief while I was out of town to grab one. Thank you for loving these characters like you do.

SYNOPSIS

When I realize I'm falling in love with my boyfriend, I decide to reveal my true self to him before we take our relationship to the next level.

But it turns out shifting into a big brown wolf in front of your very human boyfriend might not go exactly as planned.

His world upended, he ends things, and I try to move on with my life—a task that becomes impossible, especially when he can't seem to stay away from me.

And *especially* when he can't handle seeing me with another guy.

Will Deacon realize that we, the teen wolf and the sexy human swimmer, are truly meant for each other before it's too late?

*This is a New Adult, Paranormal **M/M** Romance. It is a 20,000-word novella that takes place in the world of Blackstone Academy. You should at least have read Ben's book (Blackstone Academy Book 2) before reading this novella. It is set during the events of Ben's book and includes a spicy* *epilogue set during the events of Knox's book ten years later. As always, this novella is intended for readers who are **_18+_** because it contains foul language and explicit scenes. If you're ready to see how our sweet baby Asher got his HEA with sexy, grumpy Deacon, come on in!*

A NOTE FROM THE AUTHOR

Hello there! Just a quick note this time before we dive into Asher and Deacon's story.

While all of the books in the Blackstone Academy series are technically standalone stories featuring a different couple each time, it would definitely be best if you've at least read Ben's book (Book 2) before reading this one. As this is a novella, I've left all of the world building regarding the wolf pack, the school, the side characters, etc., to the longer books. So, if you're one of my M/M-only readers, just read Ben, then Asher, and call it a day!

Alternatively, this author is a strong believer that Asher's story is best enjoyed as Book 4, even though it technically takes place during the events of Book 2. You get to know Asher and Deacon pretty well in Knox's book (Book 3) when they are twenty-eight-year-old adults, so this novella operates like a little flashback to let us all see how the two of them were able to make it work back in their Academy days.

Finally, while our characters are still in high school for the majority of this novella, I do want to stress that they are both eighteen years old. There is explicit sex in this story, both with our characters at age eighteen and then at age twenty-eight in the epilogue.

That's all! Keeping it short for our short story. I hope you enjoy.

Until next time,

- Elizabeth

PROLOGUE

ASHER

The smell of chlorine, normally so comforting, invaded my nostrils and intensified the sick feeling that had already settled like lead in my stomach.

I pulled my goggles down over my eyes and stepped up to the block as Coach blew the whistle.

"Warm up!" he shouted, his gruff voice bouncing around the high cave-like walls of the natatorium. "Two hundred meters, breathe every three strokes!"

Since the second I'd stepped onto the pool deck ten minutes ago, I'd managed to keep my eyes straight ahead and away from the other side of the pool where the sprinters were about to warm up. But as I ascended my block and prepared to dive in, I faltered.

I peered to my right, just a quick glance down the lanes, and a small, sad whine escaped my throat.

Deacon was there, standing on his own block at the far end of the pool. He'd rinsed off before practice, as we all did, and the remnants of his shower dripped slowly down through the ridges of his broad muscular torso. His jammers clung to his strong thighs and accentuated the big, beautiful cock I'd only just begun to get acquainted with that was now taunting me.

He ran a big hand over his short-cropped dark hair, and his bicep flexed, calling attention to the sleeve of colorful tattoos that wrapped around his right arm and danced across his pec.

He'd let me trace those tattoos with my tongue not so long ago.

Before I ruined everything.

If he felt my stare, he didn't let it show, keeping his hard gaze focused on the surface of the water before he pulled his goggles down over his eyes. The tense set of his jaw and the scowl on his face was his default, anyway, so no one else knew anything was amiss.

His refusal to glance my way even for a second meant he was still determined to ignore me, and, really, I was thankful.

If I had to look into those liquid chocolate eyes, usually so soft and tender for me and *only* me, and see instead the anger, betrayal, and *fear* that had been there the last time I was with him, it would break me.

I dove into the water, ready to block out absolutely everything else around me while I focused on the rhythm of my strokes and the beat of my kicks. It was a small mercy that Deacon would spend most of practice with the sprinters on the other side of the pool or in the weight room, while I would go through the motions over on my side of the pool with the distance swimmers for the next hour.

And at least underwater, no one could see me cry.

When practice ended, I dragged my pathetic, sopping wet body under the shower for a quick rinse before wandering mindlessly toward the locker room.

My best friend, Hasan, walked silently beside me, knowing full well there was no pulling me out of this fog.

I'd lost the boy I thought I was in love with.

He broke my heart, but I broke his first.

After all, if your boyfriend suddenly shifted into a *wolf* right in front of your eyes, you too might feel as though your whole relationship had been a lie.

ONE

ASHER - ABOUT ONE WEEK EARLIER

Today was the day.

It was Deacon's eighteenth birthday, and I was on my way to pick him up from the local public high school so that I could take him somewhere special to celebrate.

His school was a short five-minute drive from mine, but it may as well have been on a different planet. I went to Blackstone Academy, home to the wealthiest of Shreveport-Bossier's high school students and pride of the town's elite. It also happened to be where every wolf shifter teen from our Pack attended class, rich or poor. The Alpha of the Northwest Louisiana Pack provided all shifter students with a scholarship to attend Blackstone because the Pack had faculty sprinkled throughout the school to provide us with some specialized education—all under the unsuspecting noses of the humans and the Board of Trustees who ran the school.

The public school, on the other hand, was smaller, rougher, and very much devoid of the supernatural.

I pulled into the small student parking lot at the school,

and I waited for Deacon to emerge from the large faded-brick building. The shrubs that lined the school's entrance had seen better days, looking as though they'd succumbed to the heat of the long Louisiana summer and were likely not going to make it through this scorching September. I noted that the graffiti that adorned the old gym wall had been added to since my last visit.

Deacon came stalking through the doors, flanked by a couple of his usual crew—his best friend, Darren, who I knew from our club swim team, and another who I recognized as one of Deacon's neighbors. They chattered away next to him, animated and excited about whatever the topic of conversation was, while Deacon as always remained stoic and unmoved.

His scowly face was so sexy, and I had to swallow through the jolt of happy nerves the hard set of his jaw and cold glint in his eyes always elicited in me. That scowl had turned me into a puddle of lust and hormones the first moment I laid eyes on Deacon at the pool—I could hardly even look at him without expiring on the spot. Somehow the blushing, stammering mess I'd become around him hadn't put him off, and I thanked the Moon every day that he'd decided I was his.

He spotted my old Prius lingering near the front of the lot, and he gave a quick nod to his buddies before slowly meandering my way, hands jammed casually in the pockets of his worn jeans. I loosened my uniform tie as he approached, thankful I'd already shed my maroon academy blazer because—*was it getting hot in here?*

This cursed shifter libido of mine. It was tired of my holding back with him. Tired of the care Deacon took with me as I came fully into my sexuality and began to explore things.

Tired of my guilt over the secrets I kept from him.

Well, you're finally going to get your wish, you animal, I told my wolf.

And my dick.

Because, if all went well tonight, I was *finally* going to lose my virginity to my sexy human boyfriend.

"Hey, Ash," Deacon murmured as he slid into my passenger seat. He leaned over to give me a rough possessive kiss that had me sweating. "I hope you haven't planned anything too big of a deal. You know I don't care about my birthday."

I hummed. "*I* care about it, Deke. So, can you play along, just for me?" I gave him my best puppy dog eyes.

He glowered at me, but a smile threatened the corner of his luscious mouth. "I'll try. Since we weren't officially dating back when it was your birthday, this can be *your* present."

Even though I was a junior and he a senior, I was actually older than Deacon and had turned eighteen way back in January. Deacon thought I was a year behind because I'd had mono and missed a bunch of school in eighth grade, but really, I'd sat out a year just like every shifter kid did when we got our wolf halves near puberty. We had to learn to control the urge to shift, and we certainly couldn't do that sitting in school with our human friends.

I huffed out a laugh. "Fine. I thought you'd at least be excited to finally see where I live?"

He raised a skeptical eyebrow. "Taking me out to your weird gated commune is my gift?"

Little did he know, we didn't let just any old human access Pack territory. The locals thought it was just a giant gated residential neighborhood with very strict security standards imposed by its governing board, but really, it was our Pack's community. We had a clubhouse, a pool, a library, and a playground. We had huge mansions where the Alpha and his betas lived, and we had smaller, quaint homes for other members of the Pack who wanted to live on territory. We even had apartment complexes and dorms for younger shifters without families.

But most importantly, we had a sprawling Pack forest made up of towering pine trees and miles of room to let our wolves out to run free away from innocent human eyes.

I'd begged my parents to let me bring Deacon on territory for his birthday, and they'd relented after about a week of my incessant whining about it. His name was now on the approved list, and he was finally about to get to know the side of my life that I'd been keeping from him all these long months.

"It's just that our community has a huge private forest, and I thought we could have a little picnic together," I replied as I pulled my car out of the school parking lot and headed for the highway. I gave him my best pouty lower lip. "I made cupcakes."

He sighed, shaking his head at my antics, but he couldn't hide the tiny smile tugging at the corner of his lip. "Okay, Ash. Whatever you want."

I beamed at him before turning my focus back to the road. We made it to the Pack's front gate in short order, and I handed over Deacon's ID to the bored-looking enforcer working this afternoon. He waved us in, and I zipped my car around the historic old mansion that functioned as our Pack clubhouse and parked in the back parking lot behind the pool.

I grabbed my bag of goodies from the floorboards behind me, and I tucked the picnic blanket I'd packed under my arm before exiting the car. Deacon had already made his way outside and was looking around the property with mild curiosity, probably wondering what was so special about this place that we kept a 24-7 gate guard and strictly controlled who came and went from the community.

"Come on, handsome," I chirped, grabbing his hand and pulling him toward the tree line of the enormous pinewood forest that blanketed acres upon acres of the back of the territory.

He came willingly, enfolding my slightly smaller hand in his strong, possessive grip as we moved through the woods.

"I wasn't aware that you were so... outdoorsy," he teased after a few minutes of walking. "Where in the world are we going?"

"Just far enough so that we'll have some privacy," I replied with a wink.

A slow smirk spread across his gorgeous face, and his eyes heated. He yanked me toward him with a rough, sudden tug, and in an instant, I found myself pressed up against the nearest tree, my bag and blanket lost to the forest floor somewhere behind Deacon as he caged me with his strong arms.

"Are you planning something dirty, Asher Boyd?" He ran his nose up the column of my neck while he reached down with one hand to loosen my uniform tie. "Out here in the middle of the fucking woods where some random stranger could see us? See *you*?"

I moaned under my breath. He was going to distract me with his body, and then I was going to chicken out of everything I had planned.

He went on, growling, "You know I don't like other people laying their eyes on what's *mine*." I felt a sharp nip to my ear, and I groaned again as I felt the blood leave my brain and head straight to my dick.

"No one will be out here," I protested as he pushed up against me with his entire body, his firm grip now on my chin as he dragged his lips along my jaw. I panted, "And I'll know if anyone else comes near. Just... trust me. I'll know."

Because I could smell another wolf coming well before we'd see them.

"Okay, baby." He pressed a firm kiss to my lips. "Whatever you say."

He pulled away suddenly, and I found I could once again formulate coherent thoughts. He bent to retrieve my blanket from the ground, then he spread it out haphazardly and plopped down to recline on top of it, gesturing for me to join him. I sat, smoothing out my clothes so I had something to do with my trembling hands, and I felt my face begin to heat as he studied me with a look of amused curiosity.

"So, um...," I began, trying not to lose myself in those dark eyes. "I think you know, Deacon, how much I like you. I might even *more than like* you." We hadn't said the "L" word yet, and it was yet another bridge I'd been hesitant to cross while he still didn't know the most important thing about me. "And I've been wanting for a while now to give you... all of me."

He gave me a soft smile. "We go at your pace, Ash. No pressure, you know that."

I did. Deacon had quite a bit more sexual experience than I did—with boys *and* girls—before I'd managed to worm my way into his cold little heart and refused to leave. He'd been careful with me while I explored what it meant to be both out and in a real relationship, but after all these months, I was *so* hungry for more.

"And," he continued, "I might *more than like* you too."

My heart squeezed, and I only hoped he would hold onto that feeling when he learned what I'd been keeping from him.

"Well, um...," I said, dropping my eyes from his and instead choosing to focus on where my fingers worried at the now untucked hem of my uniform shirt. "There are some things about me that you don't know, Deke. And I just.... Because of how I feel about you, I don't want any more secrets between us."

He frowned, clearly not expecting that. "I.... Okay, Asher. Whatever it is, you can tell me."

I took a deep breath. "Do you believe in magic, Deacon?"

He snorted with a roll of his eyes. "Of course not."

No surprises there. I felt the guilt creeping in. I was about to upend his entire view of the world. And for what?

For love, you idiot.

I took a deep breath and got to my feet. I began to unbutton my shirt.

"This isn't me getting naked to hook up," I told him, noticing the heat return to his eyes as I shucked my shirt from my shoulders. He drank in my lithe swimmer's torso—much leaner than his, since he was built for sprinting—while I finished undressing. I kicked off my shoes and pulled my pants and boxers down, stepping lightly out of them. "It's just.. it'll be easier if I show you."

"I've seen you naked, Ash," he murmured. "Not sure what you could have been hiding on your body from me all this time."

I looked into his eyes that were still shining with lust as he raked them over my naked body, and I sucked in a deep breath. It was now or never.

"Please don't freak out. I'll explain everything—I promise."

I willed my wolf to come forward, and with a quick shimmer of the air around me, my body morphed. I hit the ground on all four paws, shaking out my shaggy light-brown fur, and then I turned my wolf eyes toward Deacon.

He'd gone rigid—frozen in shock, his big hands gripping the blanket underneath him, and his chiseled jaw hung open as he sucked in a few harsh, desperate breaths.

"What the *fuck*, Asher," he whispered, and my stomach dropped as he started to slowly scoot away from my wolf like he was... afraid. His voice rose. "What the fuck!"

My wolf stepped tentatively toward him. I thought maybe if I could get him to pet my head, he'd see I was still me—gentle, sweet, and head over heels for him, no matter the form I took.

But he seized up at my wolf's advance in his direction, so I stopped immediately. I restrained my wolf and shifted seamlessly back into my human form.

"It's okay, Deacon," I said, holding up my hands in surrender. "I'm still me, see? I just... have this other part of me. There's a whole community of us here who are wolf shifters."

He was still slowly scooting backward on the blanket, putting distance between us while he stared at me like I was a stranger. Nothing remained of the hint of fondness that would normally soften his hard eyes just for me.

He looked at me now like I was a scary monster.

"What the fuck," he repeated, shaking his head. "I can't...."

"Deacon, please," I begged, feeling the tears start to well behind my eyes. "Just let me explain it all."

He jumped to his feet and continued to take shaky steps backwards. "No. Stay... stay back. Stay away from me."

I felt my chest being ripped in half.

"Deacon," I sobbed. "No. *Please*."

His face hardened, and his glare seared me to my bones. "No. Fuck this. *Fuck* this."

He turned and ran.

TWO

DEACON

I sprinted blindly through this God-forsaken forest where I was apparently one wrong move away from being attacked or eaten by a giant fucking *werewolf,* and I was dead set on reaching the front gate without looking behind me. I didn't want to see Asher's face.

I could feel his heart breaking. My Asher.

I steeled myself. Not *my* Asher—not anymore. My Asher was the soft, beautiful boy who was my friend and teammate and then became so much more.

This Asher was a liar.

This Asher wasn't even a *human.*

This Asher could rip me in half with his *wolf* jaws.

This can't be real, I told myself as I exited the forest and careened around the side of the stately clubhouse that five minutes ago, I'd thought was just, like, the HOA headquarters or something equally fancy and dumb. *This is a nightmare. I'm having a nightmare.*

I slowed my sprint as I reached the front, and then I marched right on out of an unlocked side gate on the exit side of the entrance. Apparently, this freak wolf commune was Fort Knox if you were trying to enter, but no one gave a shit anymore once you were trying to leave.

I yanked my phone from my pocket and ordered a rideshare while I tried to slow my rapid breathing. The September evening air was still hot and muggy, and I felt the beads of sweat as they dripped slowly down my back. As the panicked adrenaline rush began to recede, feelings of sadness, anger, and betrayal seeped into my bones.

I should be breaking a sweat because I was celebrating my birthday by finally fucking my boyfriend into a coma like I'd been dreaming about since we first met all those months ago—back when he could only look shyly at me from under his long lashes while he blushed at my blatant perusal of his fucking adorable face. Instead, my white T-shirt was stuck to my sweaty back because I'd run away from him faster than I'd ever run anywhere in my life.

Goddamn it, Asher. Why did you have to go and ruin fucking everything?

My ride approached, and I dared a glance behind me before I ducked into the car. Nothing. Just a deceptively quiet residential neighborhood surrounded by dark woods. No Asher chasing me down to beg me to stay with him—to tell me that I was overreacting and this wasn't fucking bonkers and really, *really* not okay.

I guessed he knew, just as I did, that there was no coming back from this. He'd made me fall for him, and then he'd pulled the rug out from under my feet.

No, he wasn't my Asher.

He was... a *stranger*.

THE FIRM SLAM of the front door and my mom's footsteps in the hallway jarred me from my restless sleep early the next morning. She was just getting back from her overnight shift at the University Hospital where she worked as a registered nurse three nights a week.

I groaned, rolling over to fumble for my phone on my nightstand.

"Good morning, baby," Mom sang as she poked her head through the narrow crack of my open bedroom door. Her dark hair was in its usual post-shift disheveled ponytail, and she looked exhausted despite the pep in her voice. "How was your birthday? Did you and Asher do something fun?"

Fuck.

Asher.

I seized the tiny little kernel of hope that bloomed in my chest that it had all been just a bad dream, but it was quickly smashed to dust by a glance at my text messages.

Ash: Deacon, please. I'm so sorry

Ash: Please talk to me. I know it's a lot to take in but I didn't want to lie to you anymore

Ash: Just let me explain

"Asher and I are...," I began, not knowing what the fuck to even say to my mom about this. "Not seeing each other right now."

She gasped, her small hand flying to her pale cheek. "What? Did something happen?"

I cringed, throwing my arm across my eyes in an attempt to block out her distraught face and the world in general. "I just... found out he hadn't been truthful about some things, Mom. I'm not sure it's... meant to be."

It was as if an actual crack began to form in my heart as I uttered those words out loud.

Mom dared to fully enter my small room—usually forbidden this early on a Saturday morning—and she made her way over the side of my bed. She grasped the hand that wasn't attached to the arm I was currently hiding behind, and she squeezed.

"I'm so sorry, Deacon," she whispered softly. "I know you really felt something for Asher. I hope you'll be able to work through it, but I understand if you feel like you need to move on. I'll be here if you need to talk." She released my hand, and I felt tears begin to well before a sharp surge of anger torched them instantly. "After my nap, though."

"Thanks, Mom," I murmured.

I must have dozed off after she left my room, because the next thing I knew, I woke again to the sun high in the sky and blazing through my bedroom window, illuminating a very familiar lean figure with shaggy brown hair as he knocked quietly on the glass.

"Come on, Deacon." His soft plea floated though the ancient windowpane. "We have to talk."

No, we fucking did not.

I rolled out of bed, tossing the covers off of me in an angry huff, and stalked to the window. I didn't open it, feeling the need to keep something solid in between me and a guy I now knew could turn into a razor-toothed predator. And, anyway, I knew he could hear me through the thin glass.

He probably had excellent hearing since he was a fucking *wolf*.

"Go home, Asher," I said, my voice gruff with sleep. "We don't have anything to talk about."

His big blue eyes watered, and the crack in my heart

began to widen. I pushed the feeling away. As much as I felt the primal, basic need to open the window and pull him into my arms so he wouldn't be sad anymore, this was how it had to be.

"Deacon...," he said with a sad little sniff. "Why? You'd throw away everything we had together just because I'm something... different?"

"You're not even human!" I hissed. "I just... I don't understand how you thought this was going to work?"

"Occasionally shifters have mated humans—"

"Asher," I growled, not even wanting to know what the fuck being *mated* was. "Stop making this hard on both of us. Just... stop."

He wiped the lone tear that had escaped down his flushed cheek with the back of his hand, and then his face hardened into something like anger. "Fine," he bit out. "If you're not interested even a little bit in trying to work through this... in trying to *understand*... then I won't force you."

"Fine," I echoed, not feeling as satisfied as I should have in getting my way. "You should go."

His face fell again, and I needed him to get the fuck out of my window before I had a nervous breakdown.

"So, that's it then?" he asked, lower lip trembling.

"I...."

Shit.

I forced a nod.

We stared at each other for a long, excruciating minute.

"I see," he said, breaking the silence, his voice now flat and emotionless.

I turned my back on him so that I didn't have to see him walk away. I still felt him leave—my senses as hyperaware of him as they'd been since the day he walked onto the pool deck at our first club team practice—and then I let the emptiness consume me. I collapsed against my bedroom wall and slid down to the floor, hanging my head in my hands.

Asher was a wolf. He lived in a fucking wolf cult with other wolf people, and he'd let me fall for him all while knowing he was going to fuck up my entire universe.

It couldn't work. It *shouldn't*.

I could only hope this feeling that my heart had permanently left my body and disappeared along with Asher would pass. Eventually.

THREE

ASHER

Five days.

That was how long it had been since I'd spoken to Deacon. Five days since he'd dismissed me from his bedroom window like the past nine months meant nothing. And yet I still couldn't go five *minutes* without thinking about him. My wolf was being surly jerk too, missing Deacon just as much as I did.

"Oh, look," my friend Molly said from next to me as we walked across Blackstone Academy's lush green courtyard on our way to the gym. "There's Ben Fortune. Maybe you should... go say hi?" She gave me a cheeky wink, and I felt the heat rise to my cheeks.

"Not a bad idea, man," Hasan chimed in from my other side. "Cadence told me last period that he's definitely gay *and* single. I know it's really soon since... *everything*, but it couldn't hurt to, you know... spend some time with him?"

"You should see if he's going to Jackson's party tomorrow!" Molly added excitedly.

I was definitely blushing harder now as I eyed the back of new student and Pack-member Ben Fortune. He was gorgeous, friendly, and the complete opposite of Deacon—blond, sunny, and blindingly charming.

And most importantly—he was a wolf, and according to gossip, not a super powerful one, which meant he might actually entertain the idea of "getting to know" little old me.

"Okay," I said to my friends, resolve hardening. "Why not?"

I'd do *anything* at this point to distract myself from the hurt.

I quickened my pace until I'd fallen into easy steps beside him, both of us headed to our shifter-only Gym class.

"Hi, Ben," I said brightly, hoping my tone conveyed more confidence than I felt.

"Morning, Asher," he replied, glancing at me and wearing his usual charming smile.

I fumbled for small talk. "You excited for combat in Gym today? It's not really my thing, but it can be pretty entertaining to watch."

The fact that they made us learn basic hand-to-hand combat in our shifters-only gym class was my least favorite part of the curriculum, but I suffered through it along with the three-quarters of the class that weren't high-ranking Pack members to whom that kind of thing mattered.

"I am very excited, actually," Ben replied with a pretty feral smile. "I'm hoping to be picked for a matchup."

Weird, I thought. He and his sister were supposedly *omega* pack members—the designation given to the least powerful and least aggressive wolves.

I shook off my twenty questions about that and pushed on.

"Well, uh, so," I stammered like the nervous virgin I was as we entered the front doors of the gymnasium. "I, uh... I was wondering if you were going to the party at Jackson's house after your soccer game tomorrow?"

He turned to stare at me with a look of mild surprise—and maybe amusement, I wasn't sure.

Moons, I am blowing this.

I word-vomited some more. "I broke up with my boyfriend earlier this week, and I know it's a little soon and fast and stuff, but I was kind of hoping maybe we could hang out a little bit at the party? I haven't really gotten to talk to you that much one-on-one and I just was thinking...."

I was thinking that I need to at least *pretend* I was moving on from Deacon. I was thinking that if I could somehow get the attention of this gorgeous new guy, then maybe I would feel less broken.

I was thinking that I was going to prove to Deacon I didn't need his love.

Even if I knew that was a lie.

Ben reached over to touch my arm, a kind and understanding look on his handsome face. "That sounds great, Asher. I'll definitely be there, so how about you save me a dance or three?"

Whew, good enough.

"Yeah, definitely," I said as I blew out the breath that I'd apparently been holding the whole time. "Can't wait. Okay, see you out there!" I all but sprinted away from him before I could make more of a fool of myself.

I ALMOST LOST my nerve and decided to skip the party completely. But after enduring Deacon's ignoring me for the entirety of our early-morning club team practice for the third time this week, I changed my mind. So, when Friday night rolled around, I found myself striding confidently into Jackson French's massive house alongside Molly, Hasan, and his sister, Priya—and I was on the hunt for Ben.

I certainly wasn't the world's most outgoing party animal, but I was no stranger to a Blackstone Academy rager. I was usually pretty comfortable having a drink or two and finding somewhere to chill with my friends while we watched the rest of the partygoers get up to all manner of stupid things. Before Deacon, I'd even had my first kisses with boys in the dark corners of whichever extravagant house was that night's venue.

After Deacon.... Well, we could have been at a party on the Moon, and I'd have hardly noticed. If he was there, he was the only thing I paid attention to.

I shook Deacon out of my thoughts for the fiftieth time as I stalked through the throngs of my scantily dressed, over-cologned, and intoxicated peers.

"There he is!" Molly squealed, wildly gesturing toward where Ben and his sister were exiting the kitchen and moving into the big living room where the "dance floor" had materialized. "Go on, Asher!"

I cringed and thanked the Moon that "INDUSTRY BABY" by Lil Nas X was currently blaring at max volume through the room, making it impossible for anyone to have caught Molly's shrieking.

"Yes, I see him," I replied, gently patting her arm so that she'd put it away. "Thanks, Molly."

"We'll be in the kitchen on the hunt for the top-shelf stuff," Hasan shouted at the side of my face before he gave me a light shove toward the writhing mass of dancing students. "Just try to have some fun, man."

I swallowed, giving Hasan a look that I hoped said, "You better be back here with a strong drink ASAP," and then I began my slow weave through the crowd toward Ben. I spotted him twirling Harriet Jones in circles while they both laughed and sang along to the music.

After nearly stumbling over a random couch cushion that had made its way into the middle of the dance floor, I arrived at Ben's side. I tapped him lightly on the shoulder, and he whirled around, his bright smile lighting up the whole room.

"Hi," I said, suddenly breathless. "Do you.... Did you still want to dance?"

"Absolutely," he practically purred at me, and I melted.

He yanked me into his arms, and I quickly realized I was in way over my head. Ben could *dance*— one glance around the room told me that a large number of the girls and even a few of the guys were looking at him like they were about to start stuffing dollar bills in his pants.

We moved together easily, though, and he kept his light and flirty touches around my hips or along my back. Several songs later, Hasan finally emerged from the kitchen to shove a drink in my hand, and I gulped it down as best I could while we danced.

I closed my eyes, trying to focus only on the heat of Ben's hard body next to mine and the sultry rhythm of Dove Cameron singing "Boyfriend" so that I could pretend nothing outside of those two things existed. There was no hole in my heart left by the boy I thought I loved. There was no wolf sulking in my chest, missing his human mate.

There was no Deacon. There was only me, this song, and a beautiful new shifter student named Ben.

After a few more songs, soft fingers brushed the side of my face, and I opened my eyes.

"Having fun?" Ben asked, his hazel stare roaming curiously over my face. "You were off in your own world there."

"Sorry," I said quickly, tossing back the last of my drink and cursing my shifter blood for making it harder for me to get drunk. "I'm a terrible dance partner!"

"False. I'm having a great time with you." He reached out to twirl me like he had Harriet earlier.

I barked out a laugh, and then I said, "I'll have to try harder if I'm going to audition to be your date to the homecoming dance." I snapped my mouth shut, my eyes widening in panic.

Where the heck did *that* come from?

"Oh yeah?" he responded with a chuckle. "Well—"

"Be right back!" I yelled over the music. "Bathroom!"

Then I ran away from Ben for the second time in two days because I was apparently a total freaking mess.

I didn't know what had gotten into me. The homecoming dance was in a couple of weeks, and my lightly buzzed, broken brain must have decided all this talk about dancing was a great time to try to fill the next big Deacon void—the fact that he was no longer my date to homecoming.

Moons, Asher, you are so awkward, I berated myself as I hurried down the hall in search of a bathroom. *You dance with a guy for half an hour, and all of the sudden you're asking him out because you're so Moons-danged desperate....*

I found the small bathroom at the end of the dim hallway, and I ducked inside, moving to shut the door quickly so I could hide for five minutes and get ahold of myself.

Only the door didn't close.

"Woah, what...,"

Instead, it was shoved open again with a forceful push, and Thad-freaking-James stepped inside.

Thad James, a powerful beta wolf and best friends with the Alpha's son, had trapped me in this bathroom. He was now staring at me from behind his dark-framed glasses with the cold indifference he used to strike fear into the hearts of weaker wolves and the legions of less popular students at the Academy.

I shivered.

Why are you torturing me like this, Moon?

"Thad, uh, what are you doing?"

He leaned against the door, his arms folded across his muscular chest, and I attempted to put as much space in between us as possible—which was only another six inches until my butt hit the sink.

His voice was barely above a whisper. "Asher, I need you to do me a favor."

What? The likes of Thad James did *not* need things from people like me. Well—except that one time back during my freshman year when he snuck me into a closet at a party, and we made out for an hour. If I hadn't been certain I was into boys before that, I definitely was when he'd finished with me.

I frowned at him. "A favor? From me?"

"Indeed. You will stop whatever this shit is you're doing with Ben Fortune."

"What?" I blurted. Thad and the other Elites—Knox and Mason—did nothing but fight with Ben and his sister. They all detested each other, and for good reason. "But... why? You hate him."

"Irrelevant," he snapped.

"Thad, I...," I began, grasping for words. Other than Knox, our Alpha Heir, Thad was at the top of the food chain among the Pack students, and he could absolutely order me around. He had enough power to submit me here in this bathroom, and I could do nothing about it. I sighed. "I don't understand. We're just dancing, anyway."

Wrong thing to say, apparently. In the blink of an eye, he was on me, pressing me up against the sink. I fumbled for the edge, stopping myself before I crashed into the mirror behind me. I froze as he grasped me around the throat, his grip as firm as could be while still allowing me to breathe freely.

"You don't have to understand," he said softly, and then I felt his thumb move across my jaw like he was soothing me instead of threatening me. "You just have to remember that my word is law, and you know there *will* be consequences if I find out you disobeyed me."

This is such bullcrap, I thought as I tried to glare at him. I could only manage it for about four seconds before I had to drop his stare, his dominance overpowering me quickly.

Why Thad James cared who Ben Fortune was dancing with at a party was a mystery to me, but it was probably all part of the Elites' war against the Fortunes.

He must've felt my resignation both to his demand and to my entire screwed-up situation, because he gave me a little grin and patted my cheek. "Great, I'm glad we're on the same page. I'll leave you to do your business, and then I suggest you call it an early night."

Then he was gone.

"Why is this my life right now?" I moaned at the ceiling.

I'd been having a good time with Ben. I wasn't about to hop into bed with him, even if he'd asked—which he hadn't—but he had been a wonderful distraction from the emptiness in my chest, just for a little bit.

And now I didn't even have that anymore. Thad would make my life hell if I defied him, and I certainly didn't want to put poor Ben into the Elites' line of fire more than he already was.

I stalked back down the hall, ready to be done with this

entire night. I found Hasan playing cards in the dining room, and I quickly explained what happened. His jaw had dropped by the time I ended my story, but he shook it off and instead tried to give me his best sympathetic face. He shoved his keys into my hand and promised that Molly would come get me for breakfast in the morning.

I could only nod, and then I snuck out the side door so that I didn't have to explain to Ben why I was ghosting him like a coward.

The muggy late September night air settled around me, thick and heavy, reminding me that I was still a little sweaty from the dancing I had been forbidden to return to. I kicked a rock out into the yard as I skulked around the side of the house, headed toward the huge front field where Hasan's car was parked among a hundred others.

I hadn't gone ten feet when I found myself once again pressed against an unforgiving surface by a big, hard body. But this one I knew—intimately.

"Deacon?"

FOUR

ASHER

"Just what the *fuck* do you think you're doing?"

The sound of his deep, raspy growl shot instant pleasure straight through my entire body—the fact that he was clearly pissed off about something not dampening my enjoyment of hearing his gruff voice again even a little.

I allowed myself a few seconds to bask in the feeling of his taut chest pressed up against mine and his lips so tantalizingly close to my ear before I mentally slapped myself. He had no business being angry with me for *anything* I may have been doing tonight—not to mention the fact that it was kind of insane that he was at this party in the first place.

I pressed both hands into his chest and forced him back a step, and then I put on my best scowl.

"What are you talking about, Deacon?" I huffed. "I'm not sure why you think anything I do is your business anymore. Why are you even here?"

"I came with Darren," he stated matter-of-factly, like it made any more sense that his best friend would attend a Blackstone Academy party when he went to the public school with Deacon. He added, "He's trying to fuck Christine."

"Oh," I replied, lamely. Christine went to school with me and was on our club swim team, and Darren had been panting after her for a while now. I crossed my arms and tried not to melt under the very angry but also very sexy smolder Deacon was laying on me before I grumbled, "Did you not expect me to be at this party? Am I supposed to be holed up in my bedroom, still crying over you?"

It really was a miracle of the Moon that I wasn't, but he didn't need to know that.

"No," he bit out through gritted teeth. "I expected you might be here, and I tried to give you space by staying on the back patio. But what I did not expect was that I'd see you through the window with your hands *all over* some other fucking guy."

I somehow managed to rein in the smirk I felt itching at my lips. Deacon was definitely here to check up on me, and now he was *jealous*.

Instead, I let the other more appropriate emotion I was currently feeling—righteous indignation—shine through. I snapped at him, "Screw you, Deacon. You *dumped* me! I can touch as many other guys as I want to."

He growled and caged me against the side of the house again. I let him do it, too, because even though he was taller and more muscular than I was, I was still a wolf shifter with slightly enhanced strength in my human form.

But I liked what he was doing to me, so I didn't fight him.

I wasn't proud of it.

"I did not *dump* you," he rasped as he glared at me with those deep chocolate eyes. "You lied to me. You broke us. And now apparently you're just going to let some other asshole grope you in front of your entire school like you belong to him."

"Ben was not *groping* me, you ridiculous—"

"Oh, is *Ben* a wolf like you? Are you going to let him fuck you, too, because you can be *mates* or whatever the fuck it is you wolves do?"

"Deacon, nobody is *fucking* me—"

"You are goddamn right," he barked. "Nobody is fucking you, and I am going to go inside that house and break every finger on *Ben's* hands for having them where they do not fucking belong."

Moons, the war inside of me at this moment. I was so furious at the *audacity* of him, while I was also more turned on than I had ever been in my entire short life.

"Don't even think about it, Deacon," I retorted. "Ben *is* a wolf shifter like me, which means he is stronger than you are. Don't try to pick a fight with him, because you will lose."

"I knew it," he growled. "You've been such a little tease, Asher. Making me feel with every fiber of my being that you were *mine* when you knew you weren't meant for someone like me. Making me want to *destroy* anyone else who touches you when you knew I couldn't really have you. And now you're just rubbing it in my fucking face!"

That was enough, so I shoved him off of me again, this time with some real force. His eyebrows shot up as he realized I'd been holding back with him all these months.

I pointed an angry finger in his face. "I *was* yours, Deacon. Don't blame this on me. You ran away. You were the one who was too scared to face something new and different, for me—the guy you supposedly feel *this* strongly for. Stop blaming this on me, and stop acting like I'm doing something wrong by trying to move on from—"

He slammed his lips into mine with a pained roar, and I couldn't smother the moan that escaped me as he shoved his tongue into my mouth. I opened so wide for him—purposefully reminding him that I could open wide for other parts of his body—and he gripped my face so hard, it would have bruised me if I wasn't a shifter. He smashed me up against the wall with his entire body, and I could feel his dick rubbing right up against mine, the thin layers of our jeans doing nothing to mask how painfully hard we both were.

He devoured me, and I let him. Of course I did—I loved him, even though he was *so* out of line right now and what we were doing was definitely inappropriate and really stupid.

But I was weak for him, so I let him consume me for the shortest two minutes ever. Then I shoved him off of me, once again reminding him that I was stronger than he remembered and that he was only manhandling me because I allowed it.

"That's enough," I panted. "Unless you're here to tell me you've had an epiphany and are willing to work through all of this with me, you can leave me alone now, Deacon."

For a moment, he looked pained, but that expression was gone in an instant, and the anger reappeared. "You're a supernatural *creature*, Asher," he spat. "It's... delusional to think this could work between us."

That was what I thought.

"Right," I said with a resigned sigh. "Bye, Deacon."

Then I sprinted off toward the field of cars at top speed, refusing to look behind me, just as he had when he ran from me on his birthday.

SCHOOL WAS abuzz with juicy Pack gossip on Monday—so much so that it almost distracted me from thinking about how pathetic I'd been all weekend, holding onto a tiny little sliver of hope Deacon would text me and tell me how wrong he'd been and beg me to come back to him.

He didn't, of course.

"Yeah, apparently Mave's wolf is so powerful, she submitted Nikka Parker and four of her friends all at once," Molly whispered conspiratorially to Hasan, Priya, and me as we were huddled near my desk before the start of our sixth period Responsible Shifting class. "Hadley told Bailey who told me last period that Mave and Ben are, like, *real* Alphas. They may even be as strong as Knox!"

This was all just the cherry on top of how pathetically embarrassing I'd been acting. Not only had I continued to mope around over Deacon all weekend, I'd also apparently tried to ask an honest-to-Moon *Alpha wolf* to be my date to the homecoming dance.

And then I'd ditched him because I was afraid of Thad and incorrectly assumed Ben would have felt the same way I did.

I was such a mess.

Conversation ceased as Ben entered the classroom. He looked the same, with an easy-going smile affixed to his handsome face while he ran his eyes lazily over the class until he zeroed in on where I stood behind Hasan and Molly.

Crap. Is he mad at me? Hasan had definitely told him that I had made me leave that night, but it didn't mean he wasn't put out with me.

Hasan, likely sensing my nervousness, decided to be a dumb hero and stepped in front of Ben like he was going to have some stern words with him—an *Alpha*.

Ben's smiled dimmed, replaced with a look of concern as he stopped in front of Hasan. "Relax, dude. I'm still me, nothing's changed."

Hasan, bless him, pressed on. "I... I don't know which of the rumors are true, or if any of them are, really, but apparently you are *not* an omega pack member. I just want to make sure you don't do anything to hurt Asher. He had no choice to do what he did at the party."

Ben's eyes widened in shock, and he honestly looked a little crushed. "Hasan, I would *never* do anything to hurt Asher. You've known me for weeks now. How could you think I would hurt any of you?"

I listened as Molly and Hasan both interrogated him some more about whether he would even deign to be our friend anymore instead of falling in with the Elites and the other "top wolves" before Ben had clearly had enough.

He looked at me and said, "We're going to talk after class, okay?"

I mustered a nod, and then we all watched as he decided to command the front of the classroom and give us all a lecture about what really happened the night of Jackson's party. He confirmed the fact that he and his sister, Mave, were actually true Alpha wolves and that he did not consider himself above any other member of the Pack because, and I quote, "Pack hierarchy is stupid."

Hasan seemed satisfied, but it didn't stop him and the rest of my friends from flanking me on my way out the door after class ended like I needed a wall of people between me and Ben, who was waiting for me in the hallway. After I gave each of them a pleading look, they left us, and I turned to him.

I did owe him an apology. I just hoped he didn't think I was... weak.

"Ben, I... I'm really sorry about Friday night," I said, choosing to stare at my feet like the coward I was pretending not to be. "I just... I wasn't really in a place to say no to him, you know?"

"I know," he replied with a kind smile. "I absolutely am not mad at you, Asher. I get it. I had it out with Thad when I found out what he did."

Now that we all knew Ben was an Alpha, that statement worried me a lot less than it would have before. I just hoped Thad got a good taste of his own medicine.

I sucked in a breath and decided to just go all in with my show of moving on from Deacon.

"I know we were kind of talking about the homecoming dance and stuff, but I mean, now that I know who you are, I wouldn't presume...." I wanted to give him an easy out if he wasn't interested.

"Stop it right there," he said, lightly grabbing my arm. "You think that just because I'm actually an Alpha I wouldn't be interested in being your date to the dance?"

Where was this guy from? Of course I thought that—Alphas didn't just *date* pack nobodies like me.

"Well, yeah?"

"That's nonsense, Asher. You heard what I had to say in class. That's not how my family operates."

Hope bloomed in my chest, but it was mixed with guilt. I was nowhere near over Deacon, yet here I was, throwing myself at Ben Fortune.

With a tentative smile, I just said, "So, you don't have a date to the dance?"

"I would love to go with you to the homecoming dance, Asher," he said, beaming at me. "But I want to be very honest with you. I don't think I'm in a place right now to take things any further than that between us. Is that okay?"

He was apparently an Alpha wolf *and* a mind reader, because that was perfect.

"That's okay, Ben," I said emphatically. "I mean, I only just got out of a pretty serious relationship, like, a week ago. I think just hanging out with my hot friend with no expectations or pressure sounds great."

As we parted ways after that, I was in a daze. I couldn't believe I was going to the homecoming dance with an actual Alpha wolf, and I also knew that if Deacon found out, he was probably going to be... really angry.

Good.

FIVE

DEACON

The cold metal of the natatorium's bleachers dug into my ass, and I was already tired of the cloying stench of chlorine with hours still to go at the meet. The echoing shouts of the crowd and the teams and the coaches at their swimmers were making my fucking head hurt. My hair was still damp from my last race, and my club T-shirt stuck to my chest, the humidity of the natatorium clinging to my body in a familiar way that today, for some reason, I just really hated.

It was all making me even more of a moody motherfucker than I already was.

I'd won both of my races—the fifty as well as the one hundred-meter free—and I should've been feeling awesome about that and looking forward to fucking around for the rest of the day. Instead, I was perched up here at the very top of the stands, simmering with tension while my eyes were glued to Asher's agile form as he cut through the water with perfect, graceful strokes. He was halfway through the eight-hundred-meter race, and I hadn't looked away from him even once.

"I'm still not sure I understand why you guys broke up," Darren muttered from next to me, clearly noticing my torment. "I feel like you should just... go fix it."

He was put out with my bad attitude because it was interfering with his ability to enjoy the fact that he'd successfully gotten into Christine's panties last weekend at the Academy party. They were still *talking*, or whatever, and it was obvious he was trying to downplay how pumped he was about it to avoid rubbing his good fortune in my face while I was... going through some stuff.

"I can't just *fix* it," I snapped at him for, like, the fifth time. "I told you. He lied to me about some things I can't really talk about. Big things."

Understatement.

Darren sighed. "Did he apologize?"

Profusely.

"Yeah, I guess."

"Did he have a good reason for lying about whatever it was?"

To keep the secrets of a supernatural race unknown to us throughout humanity's entire history.

"Maybe."

He gave me some judgmental side-eye. "It just seems like you're... not exactly trying very hard to move on from him. Whatever happened was just so sudden and shocked the hell out of all of us. You two were couple *goals*. I just think you should be open to talking to him again."

I grunted. Darren didn't exactly know that I had, in fact, talked to Asher again since we'd broken up, nor was he aware that it had ended up with me shoving my tongue in his mouth and grinding my dick into him.

I'd known when Darren begged me to go to a Blackstone Academy party with him that there was at least a chance Asher would be there. And of course I should have said no. Keeping the distance between the two of us was the only way either of us were going to move on. Darren had whined some more, so I told myself that if Asher was there, it would be an opportunity for me to at least see that he was okay, surrounded by his friends, and living his normal life again.

So I went.

And I discovered that apparently *I* was the one who was not doing okay.

The bone-deep rage I felt seeing Asher all over some other guy had almost ended me where I stood. The fact that the guy in question was hot, jacked, and the polar opposite of me with his huge smile and dumb fucking coiffed blond hair was a hard kick to the nuts that had me so livid I almost blacked out.

I couldn't help what happened next—the intense and all-consuming desire to remind Asher that he did not belong to *that guy*. I'd known Asher was mine since the second I laid eyes on him, and I'd learned the hard way at the party that those feelings hadn't even *begun* to recede, as much as I'd been determined for us both to move on from each other.

I'd thought that maybe after enough time, I'd somehow be able to forget that there were people who could *turn into wolves* in my fucking town, and then my life could just continue on like everything was normal.

I'd even dared to think that after enough time, it wouldn't *rip out my soul* when Asher became "mates" with one of his own kind.

But now... I wasn't so sure.

Darren nudged me with his elbow and gave me a questioning look, interrupting my ruminating.

"It's complicated, man," I said with a hard sigh. "I don't know how we would just 'talk through' this... issue."

"Fine, be miserable then." He stood, slinging his swim bag over his shoulder. "I'm going to congratulate Christine on her race."

Then he stomped off down the bleacher stairs.

Thankful for the end of the interrogation, I resumed full focus on Asher as he swam the final lap of his race. He'd pulled ahead of two of the swimmers he'd trailed for most of the race and was now looking like a lock for second place. I found myself thinking about how pleased he was going to be with that finish before I remembered I wasn't supposed to be thinking about things that pleased Asher anymore.

Fuck me, I hate this.

Still, I continued to watch him like an unhinged stalker as he finished his race. He pulled off his goggles and checked the scoreboard for his time—a personal record for his eight hundred, I knew—and then I soaked in his elated smile like a drug addict finally getting that next hit.

I'd barely registered that I'd gotten to my feet before I was meandering down the stairs and across the pool deck, drifting toward the locker rooms in Asher's wake as he headed back to shower and get dressed.

I waited outside the boys' locker room, leaning up against the wall and playing with my phone like I wasn't at a complete loss as to why I was down here. I had no plan except to see Asher alone before we all boarded the bus back home, on which I was certain he was going to ignore my glare at the back of his head for all four hours of the drive—just as he'd done on the ride down.

When the last swimmer exited the locker room and there was still no sign of Asher, I slipped inside the door.

I spotted him instantly in the back corner of the locker

room, standing at an open locker with only his team-issued black sweatpants on. He faced away from me while he toweled off his shaggy brown hair, the lean, defined muscles of his back flexing with every movement. I traced every freckle on his tanned skin with my greedy eyes as I crept closer, pausing to lean up against a vacant locker a few feet away.

He blew out a breath, his shoulders bunching with tension as he let the towel drop around his bare shoulders. "What do you want, Deacon?" He didn't turn around.

I just stood there, silent, as I continued to stare. I didn't have an answer, anyway, because I had no fucking idea what I wanted.

"You just want to keep torturing me, is that it?" he huffed as he pulled on his white club T-shirt, his movements jerky, like he was pissed off. "Break up with me, then go all caveman when I try to move on, then ghost me again, then corner me in an empty locker room. Do you just enjoy messing with my head?"

I sighed. "Ash...."

He finally whirled around to face me, his cheeks flushed and a frown marring his beautiful face. "Don't you *Ash* me, Deacon. What's your problem now? Did Darren finally tell you that Hasan told him that I'm going to the homecoming dance with Ben next week? Are you here to forbid me from hanging out with another guy again, even though *You. Dumped. Me?*"

Oh, Darren and I were going to have some *words* later.

I felt every ounce of the delicate calm I'd been clinging to rush from my body as rage and *pain* surged in to replace it.

"Don't you fucking *dare*, Asher," I growled.

He scoffed. "I think I will *dare*, Deacon." He shrugged

on his backpack before he took several deliberate strides toward me, not stopping until we were nearly nose to nose. He jammed his finger into my chest, furious, and I felt again how much stronger he was than I'd known. "I begged you to come back to me. To open up your mind and try to understand how we could still be what we were, even though I'm a big scary wolf. And you refused. You continue to refuse. So, I'm going to try my very best to move on. I won't carry this broken heart around forever, Deacon. I can't!"

He was breathing hard now, seething right in front of my face. I swallowed, willing myself to calm down—to shove away the fury I felt at him going on a date with *Ben*. I felt my fists clench, my nostrils flare, and my body tense—the urge to pounce riding me hard. I wanted so badly to shove him against the lockers, rip his sweatpants down to his ankles, and just fucking *own* him.

But he was right. I was fucking this all up—and apparently I couldn't stop.

"Do not let him touch you," I managed to hiss between gritted teeth. "Just... not yet."

I'm not ready.

Disappointment flitted across his face for a fraction of a second before the anger returned. "Screw you, Deacon."

He pushed away from me and stalked out the door, leaving me to collapse against the wall in utter defeat.

He didn't look at me once for the rest of the meet or on the long drive home.

SIX

DEACON

Things were not improving for me. This was evidenced by the fact that I was currently sitting on the ground, partially obscured by a clump of bushes, while I spied on Asher like a fucking psycho creeper.

I'd had five days since our weekend swim meet to get my head on straight—with no success.

I had one day until the ticking time bomb that was Asher's homecoming *date*.

So, here I was. Just sitting on the ground at Blackstone Academy.

I'd parked my beat-up Explorer around the block before sneaking onto campus right around the time Asher would normally finish up swim practice with the school team. At a complete loss as to what I was even doing or why, I'd plopped onto the grass to brood while I twirled an unlit joint through my fingers. It had been given to me by my neighbor, Evan, who shoved it into my pocket before I left school earlier this afternoon. I could see most of the student parking lot from my hiding spot, and right on time, students began to trickle out to their cars as their sports or after-school clubs came to an end.

It was only a few minutes before I spotted Asher meandering into the lot with an easy smile on his face while he talked with Hasan. They were headed toward Asher's little white Prius, but then they diverted over toward another group of students gathered around a black Tesla.

I released an involuntary growl as I spotted *Ben* in that group—with his perfect hair and broad chest and golden tan—and Asher just trotted right on up to him with a big, beaming smile on his face.

Fuck *this*.

The slamming of a nearby car door startled me out of my murder plotting.

"Hey, man, are you, uh... okay down there?"

I looked up to see yet *another* extremely attractive guy ambling toward me, having just slammed the trunk of what looked like a very expensive BMW. He was wearing a Blackstone Academy Soccer T-shirt and black sweatpants, and his dark hair was still wet, hanging into bright green eyes that were currently taking me in with a mix of curiosity and concern. He was tall, muscular, and had as many tattoos as I did, the bright colors crawling up both of his arms and bleeding onto his chest, visible through his white shirt.

In other circumstances, I might have recognized him as a kindred spirit, but he had that look about him I'd begun to recognize from Asher and his friends as potentially something *other*. I huffed out a frustrated sigh at his approach, shifting my menacing glare back over to where Asher was still just chatting away at Ben like he was the most interesting fucking person in the world.

The new guy came to a stop in front of me. I glanced up

at him to find him peering down at me curiously, and then I watched as he craned his neck around to try to figure out what I'd been so focused on in the parking lot.

His eyebrows rose as a look of understanding hit his face. "Oh."

"Are you one of them too?" I muttered, staring at Asher again. "You should probably fuck back off to your *pack*."

I knew enough to understand that I shouldn't be out here, rambling about wolves to strangers, but I figured the risk was low—if he wasn't a wolf, he'd just think I was nuts and hopefully leave me alone.

He just chuckled knowingly, and my stomach pinched.

Another hot-as-fuck wolf guy who goes to school with Asher. Cool. Perfect.

And of course, because I was being tortured, he didn't fuck off. Instead, he just dropped down next to me in the grass, reclining lazily as he joined me in staring at Asher and the others where they were gathered.

"You see that girl over there?" he said breezily, like we were old friends just shooting the shit. "The gorgeous blonde with the french braid and the purple tank top?"

I nodded. She was hard to miss because she was indeed stunning. She was huddled in the group, leaning up against the Tesla and talking to a shorter Black girl with cropped bleached blonde hair. The tall blonde also looked suspiciously similar to Asher's homecoming date, the realization of which brought a fresh scowl to my face.

My new friend rambled on. "That's Mave Fortune. The guy you have been trying to murder with your eyes from over here is her brother, Ben Fortune. They are both, as you say, *one of them*. Mave is a powerful Alpha wolf—in all likelihood, the most powerful female in the entire Pack." He paused to pluck the joint from my hand, raising it to his nose to give it a little sniff, then he nodded his approval as he handed it right back to me. "She's also my girlfriend."

"What's your point?" I asked, back to sullenly watching Asher and trying to will him away from *Ben Fortune* with just my mind.

"My point is, I'm human. I can't turn into a wolf. But I love her, and she loves me."

He *maybe* had my attention now.

I turned to look at him. "And you're just... okay with all of this? Your girlfriend tells you she can turn into a fucking wolf, and that there's a whole community of people like her in this town—in the *world*—and you were just like, cool, I'll roll with it?"

His expression turned sympathetic. "Look, I'll admit the existence of supernatural beings was not as big of a shock to me as it likely was to you, if I'm guessing correctly as to what's going on here. I, uh... had a wolf shifter in the family a few generations back. But it doesn't mean I don't understand what it feels like to love someone who is from a *very* different world than I am."

I eyed him. "You're not worried she's going to leave you someday for another wolf? That your differences won't just end up driving you apart?"

He was thoughtful. "I mean, I can't predict the future, right? All couples have challenges. But I do know that if Mave ever left me, it wouldn't be because I'm not a wolf. All I know for certain is that I love her, and I'm going to give our relationship everything I have and pray it's forever."

Something bloomed in my chest then. Just a tiny, soft flicker of something that felt a little bit like hope.

"I just...." I trailed off, suddenly feeling pretty fucking pathetic. I whispered, "This scares me."

He reached over to clap me on the back, because apparently we were best fucking friends now. "I know, dude. And it's still so new, right? You'll need a lot more than a few weeks to process it all. But don't you think Asher is worth at least trying for?"

I swallowed. Of course he was.

What the fuck was wrong with me?

He continued, "You may not believe it, but there are wolf-human matings and marriages. They do happen, and many of them go on to live happy, long lives together. And you've seen how integrated the shifters are into the human world anyway. It's doable, man. Believe in it. I know I do."

The sincerity in his tone got an actual laugh out of me. "Sure thing. Thanks...?"

"Blake," he replied to my unspoken question, sticking out his hand.

"Thanks, Blake." I shook his hand. "I'm Deacon."

"Nice to meet you, Deacon. Think about what I said. Hopefully, I'll be seeing you around."

He stood then, dusting himself off before he hopped off the curb and turned to face me again. "Well, I'm off to bury myself inside my hot wolf girlfriend."

I groaned. "Not helpful, man."

His broad grin was amused and a little conspiratorial. "Just a little more incentive for you. Fucking a wolf is... next level. Maybe you knew that already, but something tells me you maybe weren't quite there yet. I'll keep my fingers crossed for you."

"Thanks. I think."

"Anytime." He turned away, tossing a "Later, dude!" over his shoulder as he ambled off down the sidewalk toward his friends.

I watched him go, relieved to see that Asher had finally drifted back over to his car where Hasan and their other friends were hanging out and away from Ben. I stayed where I was, sprawled out on the soft grass and still partially hidden behind a bush like a total weirdo, and I took the time to absorb Blake's words.

My feelings of betrayal at being blindsided by Asher's *real* self had ebbed some over the past few weeks, if only because I understood why he wouldn't have wanted to expose such a major secret to anyone he was dating until he knew it was serious. It still stung, feeling like I'd fallen in love with a lie, but I couldn't deny that Asher was still Asher—the idea that he'd somehow now feel like a total stranger to me having flown out the window the second I saw him again at that party.

But could I really become a part of his world? Blake seemed to think it was simple, but I wasn't so sure I shared his confidence.

He was right about one thing, though—Asher *was* worth trying for.

And I was being a fucking dumbass because I was afraid.

Of... magic and shit.

Long after the parking lot had cleared and the warm October sun had almost fully set, I finally made my way back to my car. My thoughts were jumbled, my feelings uneasy, but I found myself feeling confident about at least one thing.

Asher was *mine*, and if he thought I was going to let another guy put his hands on him again, he had another thing coming.

After I parked my car in front of my house, I pulled out my phone and sent a text.

Me: We need to talk

SEVEN

ASHER

My phone buzzed in the pocket of my suit pants, startling me out of the pleasant conversation I was having with Ben as he drove us toward the Academy. I was growing frustrated at the interruptions, and it took my full concentration to keep the bright smile on my face and *not* yank my phone out to read the latest from Deacon.

It was Friday evening, and I was on the way to the homecoming dance with my very hot date. Ben looked like he'd just stepped out of a magazine, wearing a fitted navy suit, pale pink dress shirt, and a loosened blue tie that gave him a sexy, disheveled look. I was pretty proud of my own slim-fitting dark gray suit, white shirt, and red tie. My parents weren't as well off as those of most of my classmates, but my mom's job working for the Pack as an accountant allowed us to splurge on nice things when needed, and she'd been so thrilled to get me this custom suit for my dance. I'd even gotten my hair to behave.

And I'd left Deacon's sudden requests to talk—one from

last night and one this morning—on read. I just didn't know what to make of them.

My phone vibrated again as Ben pulled his car into the Academy's student parking lot. He really was a saint for pretending like he hadn't noticed how much my text messages had been interrupting our drive.

We parked next to Blake's car, and we found him, Mave, Harriet, and her date, Tyson, all standing around, waiting patiently for us. Ben hopped out and trotted around to my side of the car, and he opened the door with a flourish, offering me his arm. "Ready?"

I snorted a little giggle at his chivalry, and as I stood and grabbed his arm, I vowed to push Deacon out of my head and enjoy the rest of this night.

We marched into the gym, finding the lights low and the Academy's black-and-maroon school colors hanging from floor to ceiling and sparkling on every table. I gripped Ben's arm tighter, battling a fleeting moment of self-consciousness at the attention our group drew from the crowd of students as we entered. Ben and Mave had become minor celebrities in the Pack, and even the human students could tell there was something magnetic about them both. I'd always just blended right in, being no one of note, and catching even a sliver of the rays of Ben's limelight was not something I was used to—not even a little bit.

We meandered to some tables along the perimeter of the gym, and I settled into chit-chat with one of Mave and Harriet's human friends and her date while my phone continued to burn a hole in my pocket.

I felt a tap on my shoulder. "I'll get us some punch," Ben said into my ear, and I gave him my biggest smile before he wandered away.

I watched him go, taking a moment to admire his

fantastic butt until my mind morphed that view very quickly into Deacon's similarly stellar backside, and the resulting twinge in my dick confused me greatly. I wasn't sure which guy was the one that was currently turning me on.

One more buzz against my leg, and I lost the battle. I pulled my phone from my pocket and read over the text conversation, beginning with the message from last night and ending with the one sent two seconds ago.

Deke: We need to talk.

Deke: I'm serious, Asher. Stop ignoring me

Deke: I know you're going to the dance tonight, but I really need to see you

Deke: Please, Ash. Please?

Deke: I'm sorry. For everything. Please don't tell me it's too late

That last one really punched me in the gut. I'd been ignoring him, thinking he was just going to try to screw up my date with Ben because he was jealous, but the tone of the later texts had me... daring to hope?

Too late for what, Deacon? To fix us?

The thrumming beat of the music and the hum of chatter around me faded into the background as I stared at my phone, willing it to give me answers.

"Everything okay?"

Ben was back, and I shoved my phone into my pocket while I tried to act cool. He handed me a cup of red punch that I was disappointed to find did not contain any booze when I took a sip.

"Yes, yes," I said hurriedly. "It's nothing, don't worry. I'm fine."

Very convincing, Asher.

He wasn't buying it, but he was a gentleman about it, at least. After giving me one last concerned look, he turned his charming smile back on as he asked, "Wanna dance?"

That sounded like a good plan. "Yes, please."

So, for the next hour, I let myself get lost in the music and the crowd and in Ben, who hugged me tight a lot of the time, but it felt more comforting and playful than overtly sexual—somehow exactly what I needed. When it was time to take a break, he grabbed my hand and a couple of waters and lead me to a vacant table in a quiet corner of the gym. He looked at me again with some worry, and I had begun to feel guilty enough that I was considering coming clean about what was going on.

Before we could sit, someone came up behind us, and I recognized his familiar scent immediately.

"Ben, may I have a minute?"

We both turned, neither of us surprised to find Thad James there, his eyes boring into Ben with a look full of so much longing and devotion that I felt my *own* stomach flip.

Because that was how Deacon had always looked at me.

A few pieces of this particular puzzle snapped together, and I had to smile to myself.

Of course.

"Asher," Thad began, and it was clear from the tense set of his jaw that he was just a *little* irritated with me for ignoring his edict to keep away from Ben—something I had become much more comfortable with once I'd learned Ben was an honest-to-Moon Alpha wolf who wouldn't be putting up with any of Thad's nonsense. "I apologize for interrupting, but I need to—"

I held up a hand. "Let me say something before you go any further, please, Thad."

Ben and Thad both turned to me with looks of mild

surprise, but I thought the least I could do was put them both out of their misery.

And besides—I'd come to a decision of my own.

I turned to Ben. "Ben, you have been so wonderful tonight. It has truly been one of the best nights ever, and I want to apologize to you for being a little distracted." Understatement of the year. "If I'm being honest, my ex has been texting me for a few days now. I've been conflicted about it, but I think...." *Moons, was I being stupid?* "I think maybe I need to see him. I'm sorry if I haven't been the most focused date."

"It's been great, Asher," he replied with an understanding smile. "Don't worry about it at all, okay? You need to do whatever you need to make sure you can make the right decision about your relationship. I know the breakup is still fresh. Do you need a ride somewhere?"

"No, no," I said quickly. I refused to ruin Ben's night any further. "Please don't leave on my account. He can come get me. I'm so sorry, again."

"Stop that. You don't need to apologize."

Ben was the best, and I hoped we would be friends for a very long time.

My fingers flew over my phone to type out the world's fastest text, and then I turned to Thad.

Me: where are u?

"Thad," I said, and I couldn't help but smirk at him. I wasn't sure how I hadn't seen it before, but Thad was so gone for Ben, it wasn't even funny. "I get it now. You don't hate Ben at all, do you? Kind of the opposite?"

He bristled, definitely not used to being spoken to like that by little old me, but I had to hand it to him—he was making an effort here. "I like Ben a lot, Asher. I always have, even if it didn't seem that way," he replied, almost convincing me he was calm and collected instead of on the edge of desperation.

This was hilarious, and cute, and perfect, really. "Uh-huh," I replied, still giving him a shit-eating grin. "I suggest you don't screw this one up. Ben's amazing, and you'd be very lucky to be with him if that's what he wanted."

"Noted," he said, a little snippy and very Thad-like. "Thank you."

Because I was the nicest person ever, I decided to throw him a bone, hoping that Ben would decide that Thad deserved it.

I turned back to Ben. "I know he's not been on his best behavior, but Thad's a good guy, Ben. He's always watched out for every queer kid in the Academy and in the Pack. And, if he's as good at other things as he is at kissing," I went on, shooting Thad a wink because apparently I had a death wish? "Then I suspect you will be in *very* good hands."

"Asher, you naughty boy," Ben said with giant smile and a chuckle. "Got a little taste of King James, did you?"

Ah, I hoped Thad enjoyed that nickname, because it definitely suited him.

"It was a long time ago," I replied. "And he made me feel like it was the most normal thing in the world—liking boys. I'll always remember that."

My phone buzzed in my hand.

Deke: I'm in the parking lot

Of course he was.

"That's my ride," I announced. "Be good, you two."

I gave Ben a big hug, and then I threw myself at Thad, too, for good measure. He was stiff for a second before he relaxed in my arms, and he even gave me a little kiss on the top of my head.

"Thank you," he whispered, and I could only give him a

knowing look before I turned to leave them to wherever the night was going to take them.

I had better be in Thad's good graces forever after teeing Ben up just for him. In all honesty, the thought of the two of them together was *very* hot, so I wished them all the best.

My thoughts then turned to Deacon, and I sucked in a nervous breath. I was determined not to let his text messages, which didn't really tell me all *that* much, get me too excited.

But I was going to hear him out.

I snuck quietly out of the gym doors and into the cool night air that was chilly against my skin, which was still a little sweat-soaked from dancing. I marched toward the parking lot, my wolf lending a hand as my eyes adjusted to the dark, the campus lit only by the soft light of the lampposts that lined the sidewalks.

I loosened my tie as I crested a small hill, and the student lot came into view. There, leaning up against his old blue Explorer, was Deacon, his hands in the pockets of his tight, worn blue jeans as he watched me approach, his jaw clenched with worry.

I sped up, trotting the rest of the way to him like an excited puppy that had been missing its owner. The moment his dark eyes met mine and found no anger there, a look of such stark relief washed over his handsome face, it punched me right in the gut.

"Asher, you came," he said, breathless. "I didn't know if you would. I've been such a dick and—"

I launched myself at him, throwing my arms around his neck and wrapping my legs around his waist. He caught me easily, turning immediately to press me up against the hood of his car. I moaned, clinging to him, and he plastered his body to mine as he stuck his face into my neck and took in a few deep, shuddering breaths.

"I'm sorry," he mumbled into my skin. "I don't want to give up. I want to try."

I ran my hand over the back of his head, the tips of my fingers skimming through his short hair. "Okay, Deke. Okay...." I lost my train of thought as his lips met the sensitive skin of my throat, pressing soft kisses there on his way to my jaw. "Deacon—"

Then his mouth was on mine, his kisses surprisingly gentle and reverent, like I was fragile or going to be spooked if he pushed me too hard. I soaked it up, my body having many fewer reservations than my mind about the situation. After a few moments, it took every ounce of willpower I had to give him a firm push back so we could talk, rather than demanding he take my pants off and finish what he should have started the night of his birthday.

He responded to my signals instantly, pulling back to stare into my face with a very serious look. "Sorry. I shouldn't have done that. I know we need to talk."

I smiled at him, now tracing the chiseled lines of his jaw with my thumbs as I cupped his handsome face. "I'm the one that jumped you. I got ahead of myself, because yes, you're right. I just... I guess I was hoping that your texts meant what I thought they did."

With a decisive nod, he scooped me up effortlessly and tucked me into the passenger seat of his car. I'd barely gotten my seatbelt buckled before he was in the driver's seat, slamming the door behind him, and starting the car.

"My mom works tonight, so there's no one at my house," he said.

Perfect.

"Take me home, then, Deacon."

EIGHT

DEACON

I held tight to Asher's hand as I dragged him down the dim hallway toward my room. I'd been clinging to him since he'd appeared in that parking lot like a mirage, and I wasn't going to let him go until I knew I'd fixed things with us.

Or ever, really.

It had only been about three weeks since we'd broken up, but it may as well have been three years. I had no idea how I'd thought I was going to be able to just move on from him and go about my normal life. Asher was in my blood—in my *soul*—and he was *mine*.

The thought of letting him go, only for him to become someone *else's* made me want to burn the entire world to the ground.

We reached my room, and I pulled him inside and slammed the door.

Then I pressed him up against the closed door.

"Asher," I said with a low growl. "Stay here tonight."

That was not what I'd intended to say, but it was definitely what came out.

Fortunately, he just rolled his big blue eyes at me and chuckled. "We'll see." He put a gentle hand on my chest to push me off of him, and then he gave me a sexy little smirk as he walked me backwards until the back of my legs hit my bed. "Sit, please."

I did, though I would remind him later not to get used to giving orders when we were in my bedroom.

He gave me an indulgent smile, like he was proud of me for following instructions, and then he backed away a few steps before he dropped to the floor, curling his long legs under himself while he stared at me expectantly.

"I want to know why you've changed your mind," he said. "Assuming that's what this is about. If it isn't—if this is just about getting me away from my homecoming date— then I'm leaving, Deacon. I mean it."

"I know," I replied quickly. "That's not why I wanted to see you."

His eyebrows rose in the world's most skeptical look.

"Fine, that's not *primarily* why I wanted to see you," I amended. "I'm serious about trying to... fix this. Fix us."

His face softened as he nodded, urging me to continue.

I made sure I was looking him right in those bottomless blue eyes. "I'm sorry, Asher. I'm sorry I reacted the way I did when you revealed what you are. I know you only did it because you saw a real future for us together. I can't imagine what it was like for you, having to hide who you are from me for our entire relationship."

He was already getting teary-eyed, and I wasn't going to make it much longer without launching myself off this bed and wrapping my entire body around his if he carried on. He sniffed as he said, "We're all used to hiding who we are as we coexist with humans. But yes—the harder I fell for you, the worse it was."

"I'm sorry that I called you a liar," I added because that had been shitty of me. "I get that your... *kind* can't go around revealing yourselves to just anyone."

He blushed a little, reaching behind himself to rub at his neck absently. "It was really pushing it for me to tell you as it was. We're young, and the Pack really advises us to wait until we're older and closer to... mating. That's what we call getting married, by the way."

I'd gathered.

"And," I went on, dropping my gaze to my hands as I felt my face flush with shame. "I guess I was afraid. It didn't make sense to me that we could be together. I thought I was sparing myself future heartbreak by insisting that we both move on. And then I also wouldn't have had to acknowledge that the supernatural... exists."

Because I still didn't have my head around that, really, but I'd just decided to hope it actually sank in someday. I blew out a breath, daring a glance at him, and found him still smiling, amused at my fumbling apology, probably.

"So, what changed then?" he prompted me again.

"Well, I had a conversation with a guy whose girlfriend is like you," I replied. "He said he was just a human, too, and he encouraged me to try harder—to just believe it could work between us. He seemed so relaxed about it—kinda made me feel like I was making a mountain out of a molehill."

"Ah. Blake?"

"Yep."

He chuckled. "Blake seems like he's easygoing about pretty much everything, but yeah, he's dating the strongest female we have in this Pack. She'll get a lot of blowback if she mates with him because the top of the Pack has very strong opinions regarding how the most powerful wolves should mate. But neither of them seems to care even a little bit."

That was something that hadn't occurred to me. "Will you be facing that kind of pressure too? To mate with a powerful wolf?"

"Not really," he replied with a rueful smile. "My wolf isn't very powerful. I'm no one important in the Pack."

Well, that pissed me off. "Bullshit, Asher. You're the kindest, most loyal person I've ever met. The Pack has to value that."

He waved a dismissive hand at me. "Don't worry about that. I'm just... I'm so freaking *happy* you're open to being together again. And I know it's scary, Deacon. Maybe I shouldn't have sprung it on you like that."

"It's okay, Ash." I peered at him, feeling a little awkward about what I was about to ask. "Can I maybe... can I have a do-over?"

He stared at me for a second, and then a wide grin spread across his face. "You want to meet my wolf again? Properly?"

I nodded, shoving away the nerves that the thought of being face-to-face with a huge wolf elicited. I could do this for him.

"Okay!" He hopped to his feet, and I watched him eagerly as he began to strip off his suit, and I sent up a thank you to whatever wolf god or goddess that was in charge of him that he was here, in my room, stripping.

"Same rules as last time, Deacon," he chided as he loosened his tie. "I need to get naked so I don't ruin my clothes with the shift, so no funny business."

"Mmhmm," I said, smirking at him. Once he'd finally removed all of his clothes, I had only seconds to take in his lean muscles, his lightly tanned skin, and the neat tuft of dark hair that sat atop my favorite body part of his before the air around him seemed to flicker, and his body morphed seamlessly into a big shaggy brown wolf. He sat obediently on the small space of my bedroom floor, keeping his distance like he didn't want to spook me again.

Now that I wasn't about to pass out from shock and fear, I was able to really take him in. Familiar soft blue eyes stared back at me, and while those wolf teeth were sharp and intimidating, I could still see Asher's big, genuine smile in the wolf's face. I reached out a hand, and he padded forward until his big furry head was under my palm.

"Hey, baby," I whispered. "You're beautiful. I'm so sorry I ran from you the first time."

He whined, nuzzling into my hand again before giving me a big lick up the side of my face. Then he dropped his large head in my lap, letting me pet him for several long, quiet minutes. It was definitely a little weird. This was *Asher*, the boy I loved, and I was petting and rubbing on him like he was my pet. But he wasn't scary, or violent, or a monster—he was the same gentle soul in a different body.

"Okay," I said with one last ear scratch. "Thank you for letting me meet you. Can I have Asher back now?"

He chuffed at me, and then without warning, a naked Asher appeared again, kneeling at my feet like the most obedient boy in the world.

My dick took notice, and I willed it to slow down. I knew exactly what I wanted now, but I was determined not to fuck this up.

Reaching down to grasp Asher firmly around the arms, I yanked him up and into my lap. He straddled me, a wide, beautiful smile gracing his lips, and I ran my hands reverently along his back.

"I love you, Asher," I whispered. "I can't believe I ever thought I could be without you."

His smile wobbled, his lower lip trembling, and a tear leaked down his cheek as he said, "I love you too, Deacon. So much. Thank you for giving us a chance."

I flipped us suddenly, and he let out a little gasp as his back hit the mattress. I crawled on top of him, my gaze turning from worshipful to hungry in an instant.

"Asher," I rumbled, dipping my face low until our noses touched. "Ash...."

"I want you, Deacon," he gasped as I ground my still-clothed crotch against his naked, hardening dick. "All of you. Now."

"Yeah?" I said, giving him one last serious look. He knew what I was asking.

"Yes," he moaned, lifting his hips to grind up into me. "Take me."

Fuck. Yes.

NINE

ASHER

Deacon let out the world's sexiest groan, and then his mouth was on mine. I opened, letting him consume me, and I loved it. He didn't really know how to be gentle when it came to kissing, and that suited me just fine.

I moaned, our tongues tangling, and I started pawing at his pants—because why the heck was he still wearing them?

He swatted my hands away and reached down to grasp me firmly around my painfully hard dick.

"Did you let *Ben* touch you, Asher?" he rumbled as he gave me a firm squeeze. "Did you let him touch what's *mine*?"

"No," I gasped. "Not like that. I know I didn't exactly tell you this, but we agreed that we were going to the dance as friends only."

"Mmm," he growled. "I don't care. I don't like that you went with him at all."

I'd inform him later that in all likelihood Ben was with Thad somewhere doing exactly what we were about to do and not thinking about me even for a fraction of a second, but that was too much talking.

I was gradually losing the power of speech the longer his hand was wrapped around my cock.

"Deacon," I whined. "Take your clothes off."

"Shh, baby," he whispered as he ran his tongue along the shell of my ear. "Be patient."

He moved south, crawling down my body as his lips trailed along my chest, across my abs, and then lower as he placed a few bites and nips to my inner thigh, all while he lovingly stroked my cock. He was clearly on a mission to melt me from the inside out.

"Deke," I urged him again, and suddenly I found my legs thrown over his shoulders, my most private parts exposed to him in all their glory.

I'd only had one second to feel nervous about him seeing me like *this* for the first time before his tongue was on my hole. "Oh, my *Moon*," I moaned, thankful I could start swearing to the Moon in front of him without seeming totally nuts. "Deacon. Holy crap!"

He hummed with masculine satisfaction as he laved me, and I whined and moaned like a harlot, lost to the mind-numbing pleasure of his tongue on my ass and his hand on my dick.

"You like that?" he growled from between my legs before attacking me with his tongue again. "You like it when I own your ass with my tongue, Asher?"

"Yes, Moons, yes," I panted. "Please, Deacon."

He gave me a few more long, glorious licks, and then he pulled away, leaving me exposed and still wanting.

My whine only elicited a smug smile. "I told you to be patient, baby," he said as he climbed back over my body. He reached over into his nightstand and pulled out a little bottle of lube and a condom, and my heart began to thump even faster in anticipation. "I'll always take care of you."

He smacked a quick kiss to my lips before settling himself again between my legs. I watched as he slicked his fingers with the lube, and then he began exploring my hole once more.

We'd done this a few times—experimenting with his fingers in my ass, working up to the day I'd be ready for more, so he knew exactly how I liked it. His long, thick finger entered me slowly, and then after a minute, he added another. He worked me, gently stretching me while he stared down at me with his usual gruff intensity, but the soft love shining in his eyes was all for me, and I soaked it in like the greedy boy I was when it came to him.

"I'm ready, Deacon," I gasped as he brushed against my prostate, the jolt of pleasure rocketing through me and threatening to end my good time early.

"Mmm, not yet," he said with a sly grin, and then he dropped his head and closed his lips around my cock, sucking hard.

"Deacon!" I shouted, and he ignored me, working me once again with his fingers and his mouth until I was shaking and sobbing for him to slow down.

I wanted to come with him inside me, dang it, but I wasn't going to be able to hold out much longer

"Please, Deke," I whined. "*Please* fuck me. I don't want to come until you do."

He pulled away with a groan, and the grin he gave me was so, *so* savage.

"Say it again, baby," he purred. "Beg me to fuck you again."

"Ugh," I mumbled, my brain scrambled by the sensation

of his fingers that were now thrusting hard in and out of my ass. "Please, Deacon."

"Please what?"

"Please fuck me!"

"Mmm, the word 'fuck' coming from that little angel mouth is so damn hot, Ash."

"Deacon!" I was about to implode, and I sent a prayer up to the Moon to take me quickly if I died from pleasure overload.

He finally paused his ministrations, taking ten seconds to shuck his clothes at long last. I stared, drooling, taking in his chiseled body, his gorgeous sleeve of tattoos, and his very large, *very* hard dick that I was about to attempt to take into my body.

I shuddered, the anticipation driving me crazy. *Wolf up, Asher!*

He opened the condom and quickly sheathed that massive erection, then he slicked himself with lube while he stared down at me adoringly.

Surging forward, he pulled my legs up over his shoulders once again, and he notched his dick against my entrance. "Asher, look at me," he said softly, and I tore my gaze from between my legs to look into those deep chocolate eyes. "I love you. You're mine, and I'm yours forever. Understood?"

I could only nod, once again blinking back my tears. "I love you, too, Deacon. Forever."

He leaned down again, bringing his lips to mine, and he consumed every moan and whine that escaped from my mouth as he slowly pushed inside of me. It burned at first, but I willed him to keep going until he was finally, *blissfully*, fully seated inside of me.

He began to move, rocking his hips slowly—carefully—

his lips never leaving mine as he went.

"Yes," I hissed as he started to increase his pace, and I urged him on. I wasn't as fragile as he'd once thought I was. "More, Deacon."

"Fuck," he bit out. "Fuck, you feel good. So tight. So perfect."

I grabbed his face with two hands, and I nipped at his ear before I whispered, "Fuck me harder, please, baby."

That did it, and with an obscene groan, he began to thrust into me fast and hard while he worked my cock like the expert he was.

"Yes, Deacon, yes, yes, yes!" I chanted until I finally fell over the edge with a loud cry, my soul leaving my body and my wolf howling with the victory of being claimed by our human mate.

I felt my release coat my stomach as Deacon shouted his own. "Fuck *yes*, Ash. Fuck!"

He stilled, breathing hard, and he gently pulled out of me before he yanked off the condom, tying it off and tossing it haphazardly into the trash can next to his desk. He grabbed his shirt from the edge of the bed where it had landed, and he wiped my stomach clean before collapsing next to me and pulling me into his strong arms.

He curled around me, and I sighed with dreamy contentment as he placed a sweet kiss behind my ear.

"Thank you," he said, his breath tickling my neck. "For forgiving me for being an idiot. I can't believe I thought I could ever be without you."

"You were being pretty stupid," I replied, laughing as he pinched my side. "Thank you for being open to what I am. My wolf really likes you a lot."

"Does he? I guess I think he's pretty cool too."

He pulled the comforter up around us both, and I felt

my eyelids flutter, the exhaustion of the whole night finally threatening to overtake me.

"Love you, Deke," I murmured as I felt myself drifting off.

"Love you, Ash. Sleep. I'll still have you in the morning. And every morning after that."

I could tell he meant it, and now that he truly knew *all* of me, I couldn't wait to start our life together.

EPILOGUE

ASHER - ABOUT TEN YEARS LATER

"Great job, Sam! That's it—keep those hard kicks going until you get to the wall!"

Sam swam hard for the last few inches, his feet splashing wildly in the water behind him, and he grabbed the side of the pool like a lifeline before his little shaggy brown head popped up out of the water.

He gasped before he crowed excitedly, "I did it!"

"You sure did, buddy!" I exclaimed with a little clap.

When Knox Monroe, our Alpha, had marched onto my pool deck with an adorable five-year-old in tow and politely ordered me to give him a swimming lesson while my teams were off in the weight room for their after-school practice, I'd agreed without argument. I'd known instantly little Sam was Kady's brother—he was the spitting image of my new bestie and fellow Blackstone Academy coach—so of course I wanted to hang out with him. I also had a bit of a soft spot for our Alpha's efforts to woo our Pack's newest omega wolf, so I was here to help Knox however I could on that front.

The drama that was going to cause them both notwithstanding, of course.

So, I'd spent the last hour with Sam, testing his current abilities and helping him get more comfortable in the water than he already was. He wasn't a little swim prodigy like a lot of the guppy swimmers on the city club team, but he also hadn't had wealthy parents with the time and resources to put him in swim lessons before he could walk. He could float and move around enough to get himself where he needed to go, and I didn't think it would take much to get him in great shape if he wanted to keep swimming with me on a semi-regular basis.

When our hour was up, I helped him dry off before handing him over to his mother when she came by to pick him up. She thanked me profusely for my time and gave me a big hug before I could wave her off, desperate as I was not to mess up her lovely outfit with my wet T-shirt and swim trunks.

"Thanks, Mr. Asher!" Sam called as they headed for the doors, waving enthusiastically back at me.

"Bye, Sam!"

I watched them go, then I made my way into the vacant locker room in search of a dry change of clothes.

I'd just managed to peel my sopping wet T-shirt from my body when the door clanged open, and my husband stepped inside.

"Hi," I said brightly as I tossed my shirt into the team's hamper in the corner of the room. "Finished with weight training?"

Deacon smirked at me, those dark eyes lazily taking in my shirtless torso as he prowled toward where I was standing in front of the lockers set aside for the coaching staff. I froze, watching him avidly. He wore our usual coaching uniform of a T-shirt with "Blackstone Academy Swimming" plastered across the front and fitted black jogger pants. I could tell he'd been lifting weights right alongside our swimmers this afternoon by the light sheen of sweat that lingered on his brow.

He smelled amazing, and my wolf, who had been lazing in my chest, perked his head up.

Deacon and I had coached the swim teams at Blackstone ever since we'd graduated from the local public college where we swam for the university team and earned our Kinesiology degrees. Deacon took a year off between his high school graduation and college to work as a coach for the little kids in the city club team organization, so we were both able to start and finish our college educations at the same time.

He'd finally proposed to me, or rather, *demanded* that I marry him, after one year of us working side by side coaching the Academy's swimmers. Of course I'd said yes right before I'd melted into an emotional, blubbering mess. We had a human wedding in lieu of a true mating ceremony on Pack lands, and while my wolf considered him our mate in all senses of the word, I referred to him always as my husband. It was just one of the many easy things I did to keep him grounded in the human world so that it didn't feel as though our life together revolved around the Pack and what I was.

I was blissfully happy, and never more so than when my husband looked at me the way he was looking at me right now as he stalked closer, dark eyes full of heat and dirty promises.

"Teams are finished and dismissed," he replied. "No students left. It's just you and me, Ash."

I shivered, nervous excitement thrumming within me. We were on school property, and while we were technically not on the clock anymore, the thought of hooking up in here like we were a couple of horny students still felt so wrong and forbidden. I was *not* a rule breaker, but Deacon certainly was, and it always felt so Moons-damned good to just surrender to him.

He finally reached me, pulling me into a fierce, dominant kiss that had me moaning while his hands roamed up my abs and over my chest, ending in a firm, possessive grip around my neck.

He pulled back slightly to stare into my lust-drunk face. "On your knees for me, baby."

I dropped instantly, hitting the rough carpeted floor of the locker room with a graceful thud, that raspy growl never failing to command my body with ease. I stared up at him, eyes wide and mouth so hungry while I watched him pull his shirt over his head with one deft hand, and I whined with need as I took in the familiar broad planes of his colorful chest and his chiseled abs.

He was even more muscular these days than he'd been when we met, his time in the weight room increasing while his hours in the pool had naturally decreased now that he was coaching instead of competing. I always felt a little burst of pride every time I gazed lovingly at his tattoos because nestled among them was a brown wolf with big blue eyes. He sat right over Deacon's heart, declaring his love for *both* sides of me.

Deacon caressed the side of my face with the back of his hand. "So good. I'll always give you what you want, Ash." Then he pulled that beautiful, huge cock out of his sweatpants and murmured, "Open for me."

I did, and he fed me his dick inch by inch until I'd taken almost all of it. I reached up, grasping his firm ass in both of my hands as I bobbed and sucked, knowing I had a minute, tops, before he took total control.

"Fuck yes," he groaned as I hummed around him, his hands raking through my wet hair. "That perfect mouth. My perfect boy."

I loved being his perfect boy, and I continued to suck and work him with my tongue, squeezing his butt with my deceptively strong grip until he finally snapped.

"Damn it, Asher. Fuck."

He palmed the back of my head and began to thrust hard, and I opened wide and relaxed my throat, letting him use me like he so often desperately needed to do before he either came hard in my mouth or threw me against any available flat surface to take my ass.

I stared up at him, the tears beginning to pool in my eyes and the saliva starting run down my chin, and I silently begged him to give me his cum.

I *needed* it.

He knew it too. "Yeah? You needy boy."

The whine that escaped me as he yanked his dick from my mouth would've been embarrassing if I didn't know it actually turned him up to a hundred. He jerked me to my feet, his big hand still fisting his rock-hard cock, and he wasted no time in spinning me around and shoving me down so that I was bent over the bench that lined the bottom row of lockers. My hands hit the bench, and I hissed out a *"Yes"* as he ripped my damp swim trunks down to my ankles.

I somehow still had the presence of mind to reach into my gym bag, conveniently sitting six inches to the right of where my hands had landed, and I pulled out the little bottle of lube I kept in my toiletries bag because, well, this was not the first time this had happened, and I was nothing if not a Boy Scout.

I tossed it to him, and I heard the cap snick open two seconds before a slick finger entered me.

"Mmm," I moaned as he stretched me, quickly adding another finger, always knowing how to ride that line between pleasure and pain. "More, Deacon."

"So needy today," he chided, but I could hear the gleeful smile in his voice. It was the kind of smile my gruff husband only wore for me, and really only when he was fucking me, but that didn't make me love it any less.

His fingers retreated, and then he pushed his slick cock inside my ready hole, both of us releasing simultaneous groans of pleasure that were so loud, they probably echoed through the entire natatorium.

"Give it to me, Deacon," I demanded, and I received the hard slap to my ass I'd been gunning for with that little bit of sass.

"I'm feeling generous today, Asher," he purred as he started to move, rocking his hips slow and steadily. "I won't make you beg, because I love you, and I want to give you everything you want. Everything you need."

He started to move faster, his hips slapping against my ass, and I felt myself being wound tighter with every thrust, teetering on the edge of melting from the inside out.

"Please," I panted. "Your cum, Deacon. I want it."

"I know, baby. I want yours too."

He dug the fingers of one hand into my hip, always proud to leave his marks on my quick-healing shifter body, even if just for a few hours. Then he reached around with the other to stroke my dick roughly as he pounded into me, his pace frenzied and savage, owning me body and soul like he knew I needed.

"Yes, oh my Moon, oh holy gods, *Deacon*," I sobbed as my orgasm consumed me, my release coating his hand and the bench in front of me while my body shook from the jolt of ecstasy that flooded my senses.

Deacon's pace became erratic and his breathing labored until he shouted, "Fuck!" He groaned his release, filling me up like I wanted.

Like I *craved*.

His thrusts slowed, and I felt him drop his forehead to my back that was now slick with sweat. He pressed light kisses up my spine, and I never felt so loved as I did in moments like this, with his soft lips on my skin and his cum dripping from my body.

After several lazy minutes of this, we cleaned up, thankful for the abundance of towels available in the locker room, and we'd both managed to at least get our pants all the way back on before the door suddenly swung open.

"Knock, knock!" a familiar voice called as she entered the locker room with hesitant steps. "I just wanted to thank Asher for—oh shit!"

Kady covered her eyes immediately, her nostrils flaring. I knew her wolf was probably smelling exactly what had just gone on in here, and I let out a loud giggle as my face heated.

"Relax," Deacon said to her, completely unperturbed, as he pulled on his shirt. "We're decent. You can come in."

She lowered her hands just enough to peer at both of us over the tops of her fingers. I winked at her, even though this was just a *tad* mortifying, and she chuckled at my clear embarrassment before dropping her hands from her face.

"You naughty boys," she said, her sapphire eyes alight with amusement. "And here I thought I was the only one on staff letting a fellow coach penetrate me on school grounds."

We both snorted. The push and pull between Knox and

Kady was a constant source of entertainment for us, and that particular story had been a highlight, for sure.

Deacon sat down next to me on the bench where I was currently pulling on my shoes, and he threw his big arm over my shoulder. "You know I can't help it, Kady. He's pretty irresistible."

"Oh, I know it," she replied with a wink in my direction. "Well, I just came to thank your irresistible husband for agreeing to give Sam a swim lesson. He had the best time. Mom says he won't stop talking about you."

I blushed again, because *aw*. "It was my pleasure. I hope he comes back."

She grinned. "Count on it. Now, if you'll excuse me, I am going to leave you two to enjoy your post-fuck glow in peace. See you tomorrow."

We watched in amusement as she scurried out. I really liked that girl, and I hoped she and our Alpha managed to make it work somehow.

Deacon leaned in to kiss my neck. "That was fucking amazing, as always, baby."

I hummed, happy and sated. "It was."

"I fucking love you, you know that?"

I did, but I never tired of hearing it.

"I love you too, Deke. I thank the Moon daily that you joined me in this crazy double life I lead."

"I thank her too," he whispered, and I raised a skeptical eyebrow at him. "What? I do. I figured it wouldn't hurt to throw a little gratitude up to the celestial being responsible for putting you in my life."

Be still my heart.

"I knew you'd come around," I said with a big grin. "Ready to frolic with us in the woods yet?"

"Now you're just being ridiculous."

I giggled, squeezing his hand affectionately. I loved his grumpy ass more than anything in the world.

I'm Asher, a once-shy teen wolf who grew up to snag the sexy human mate of my dreams, and life is so, so good.

The End

If you'd like to see more of what Asher and Deacon are up to as twenty-eight-year-old married swim coaches, check out Knox's book if you haven't already!

If you aren't planning to read Knox's book (hey to my M/M-only readers, love y'all!) but want to get a glimpse of how the two of them meet and basically adopt Kady, an omega and Knox's love interest, flip to the end of this book for a few chapter excerpts!

ACKNOWLEDGMENTS

Whew, y'all. Thank you for journeying with me on this third installment of "Elizabeth didn't plan to write this book, it just happened."

Asher was always meant to be the nice boy Ben decided to get to know while Thad was being an idiot. His going back to his boyfriend during the homecoming dance was my way of gently separating Ben and him so everyone was happy and no one got hurt. And then as I was writing Knox, I dropped Asher at the front desk to welcome Kady to the Pack, 100% unplanned, and the rest is history. Deacon was an on-the-fly invention in Knox, and it made me even itchier to tell their story!

Also, real talk, I love writing M/M romance—a thing I discovered when I stumbled into needing to give Ben his own book. So, while I think we're closing the book on M/M in the Blackstone Academy world, I want to do more! If you follow me on the socials, holler at me and tell me what you'd want to see next. (If you were thinking, "More rejected mates, but make it gay," I am way ahead of you).

I'll try to keep the rest brief as I've babbled about my vague plans to write something different in the Acknowledgements of my other books, and it's time to try it. For real this time. I mean it.

But. I think Harriet is going to happen. Don't quote me. Check back again with me in 2023.

Okay! Thank you as always to my core team who keeps

me afloat on the daily—Steph, my PA and caretaker; McKinley, my editor and fierce protector of my boys; Cherie, the greatest cover artist to ever walk the earth; and David, my book buddy, Alpha reader, and answerer of all my awkward gay sex questions. I could not keep doing this without you guys!

Thanks to my beta readers for eagerly consuming my unpolished words and making me feel like they aren't total garbage—Delaney, Corina, Kaitlyn, Megan, Emma, Nicole, and Gwen.

Thank you to my husband, who continues to believe in me even though this whole "writing books" thing still seems pretty freaking random! Love you, boo.

And of course, thanks to you, the reader. If you enjoyed this novella (or, yikes, even if you didn't), it would mean the world if you would leave a review. Us indies depend on them!

ALSO BY ELIZABETH DEAR

Blackstone Academy

New Adult, Paranormal Romance

Mave Fortune: A Rejected Mates Story (*M/F*)

Ben Fortune: A Shifter Love Story (*M/M*)

Knox: An Alpha's Redemption Story (*M/F*)

Asher's Story: A Blackstone Academy Novella (*M/M*)

Harriet's Story: A Blackstone Academy Novella (*TBA*) (*M/F*)

A Knight's Revenge

New Adult, Contemporary WhyChoose Romance

Storm the Gates

Seize the Castle

Kill the King

Max & Frankie: A Knight's Revenge Novella (*M/M*) (2023)

ABOUT THE AUTHOR

Elizabeth Dear is the super-secret alter ego of a chick who just wants a little romance and adventure in her life every now and then. She's writing the books she would want to read as an indie romance fanatic and voracious reader and is developing her brand of smart-mouthed heroines, sexy supportive men, and strong family bonds. She loves ALL the tropes and only hopes you enjoyed the ride. Please follow her at the links below to keep up with the latest news.

Sign up for my newsletter! Join my reader group on Facebook! Visit my Merch Store at www.elizabethdearmerch.com

EXCERPTS FROM KNOX: AN ALPHA'S REDEMPTION STORY

FROM CHAPTER THREE

KADY

I parked my ancient Camry in front of the enormous historic mansion that appeared to be the Pack's clubhouse. It sat just inside the wrought-iron gates of the Pack's territory, its stone facade towering over the smaller buildings that surrounded it, and white columns lined the entrance to the three-story front porch.

I made my way inside to find a spacious common room with couches, chairs, TVs, several pool tables, and what looked like a bar taking up the entire righthand wall of the open, airy space. Floor-to-ceiling windows at least two stories tall made up the entire back wall, and through them I could see residential streets that forked off to the left, and a beautiful pinewood forest that went on as far as my eyes could see.

It was quiet—I spotted a loan elderly man reading the newspaper in a cushy-looking armchair—but otherwise, it seemed it was too early on a Saturday morning for a crowd.

"Hello there," a chipper voice sounded from my left. "Can I help you?"

I turned to find a sleek, modern front desk being

manned by a shifter guy with an angelic face, kind eyes, and a warm smile. I hoisted my worn leather purse higher onto my shoulder and approached him, resigned that this was really and truly happening.

I was becoming part of a wolf pack.

"I'm Kady Calloway, just arrived and checking in for the first time."

Front desk guy just smiled at me again and started scrolling on the tablet that was mounted behind the desk. I took a minute to examine him, noting the vibrant color of his blue eyes. They weren't the jewel tone of my sapphire eyes, and they definitely weren't the arctic blue of my Wolf Man tourist, but they were somewhere in the middle, maybe cornflower. He had shaggy brown hair and appeared to be athletic and strong, but he was much leaner than the group of wolf guys I'd "met" in the bar earlier in the summer.

Mom would've urged me to flirt with him since she'd taken to hoping I could find a nice wolf boyfriend now that we'd acquiesced to this life, but I'd informed her I was off men completely and never having sex again.

I'd peaked—a feat at age twenty-two—that night I let Wolf Man ruin sex for me with literally any other mortal being. Nothing was ever going to compare to that transcendent experience, so I figured I'd just go out on top.

So, Sunny Angel Face here was not gonna do it for me, and I had a sense the feeling was mutual, since he hadn't checked out my tits for even a millisecond during the time I'd been standing here.

I watched him fiddle with the tablet, and I knew the minute he found my information because those big blue eyes widened just the slightest bit before he looked up at me.

"Oh, you're the new omega?" he asked me as he examined my file, like I was supposed to know what that meant.

"Uh, sure. Maybe. Can you... tell me what that means?"

He looked at me curiously. "Were you not designated as an omega with your prior pack?"

Cool. The jig was up already, and I'd been here a grand total of three minutes. There really was no use in struggling to pretend I wasn't a total clueless newbie, and he seemed like the type not to be a dick about things. "This is actually my first-ever pack, Front Desk Guy. My mom's a human, and I don't know who my dad was other than that he gave me an extra-special little gift. So, you're gonna have to teach me the ways of pack life."

After all, I only knew what Monica had tried to explain to me in bits and pieces over all these years when we'd emailed or texted back and forth.

His eyes really went wide at that revelation, but then a big smile appeared. "You're half human? Wow! You know that's super rare? Oh my Moon, that's amazing! I'm so glad you found your way to us, Kady." He stuck his hand out to me. "My name's Asher, and I volunteer for front desk duty here at NWLA Pack headquarters one Saturday a month. I'm so excited you came in on my day."

Well, he was *adorable*. "Nice to meet you, sir," I said as I shook his hand. "So, do you think the omega thing has to do with my being half human? Monica Hayes sponsored me into the Pack, and she would've probably noted that."

He nodded. "I bet so. I'm guessing that maybe your wolf is smaller and doesn't pack too much power in the dominance department?"

"Yes. I mean, I guess? I don't go around challenging other wolves. I've only ever run into a few in my life."

He nodded again, his warm smile never faltering. "Well,

omega is just a special designation we have in our packs for the shifters who are the least powerful or may need special protection. Some omegas have trouble shifting; others may be disabled. Some just have very submissive wolves without an aggressive bone in their body. It's not a bad thing! It just means we'll watch out for you."

Well, that sounded like a good deal to me. I didn't exactly give two shits about official Pack designations—I was just here to start a new job and protect my family.

"Yep, sounds right to me. You'll have to excuse my ignorance. I'm... new."

Asher leaned against the desktop, slouching down onto his forearms, and he beckoned me closer like he was about to let me in on a secret. "My husband is a human, so I know firsthand what it's like navigating pack life for the first time. I'm happy to be your buddy."

Yep, definitely not a tits guy. "Husband? I thought you guys called them mates?"

He grinned. "We had a human wedding. He's slowly come around to, you know... the existence of wolf shifters, but it was baby steps there for a while. We're both swim coaches at Blackstone Academy, and he's told me not to clue him into which of our athletes are wolves. Wants to treat everyone the same."

"Oh shit!" I exclaimed, earning me an annoyed look from Old Man Newspaper. "I'm starting at Blackstone as the new women's soccer coach and gym teacher!"

"Oh my Moon, that's amazing!" he said with just as much enthusiasm. "We've got quite a few Pack members on faculty now at Blackstone. Even our Alpha volunteered to fill in as the men's soccer coach this season until we can find someone permanent. Much needed, since the soccer teams are loaded with shifter kids."

Which was wild to me, and it was even wilder that I'd gravitated to soccer without even knowing it was the preferred sport of the wolf folk. I was very fast, and I'd always been among the top achievers in the weight room, but no one had ever looked twice at me like I was something more powerful than the average human.

"I can't believe the Pack pays for all the shifter kids to attend this fancy school," I mused to Asher. "That's so much frickin' tuition money."

"The Pack does well," he replied. "Always has, and things have been going even better since our Alpha took over about ten years ago."

Monica always spoke highly of the Alpha as well, but I was pretty sure it was mostly because her beloved son was apparently his bestie.

"Well, new buddy, I just have a couple more questions, and then I'll be out of your hair," I said, digging in my bag for my phone. I unlocked it and handed it over, indicating he should put his number in. "First, is there somewhere around here that I can continue my self-defense training? Since I'm not going to be an asset in a wolf fight, I've tried to make sure I can at least fend for myself in human form."

This was true now more than ever, though Monica had encouraged me to learn well before I'd found myself in a situation where I thought I might actually have to use those skills to protect myself.

"Got you covered there," he replied. He typed something into my phone, then handed it back to me.

On the screen was the website of a beautiful modern-looking gym, and it was only a few blocks from my house.

"Fortune Fitness?" I asked.

"Yep. Mave and Ben Fortune are siblings and very powerful Alpha wolves. They went away to school for a while, and they just came back home a few years ago and opened this awesome gym together. They offer self-defense and other martial arts training, and I'm pretty sure Mave teaches classes for women only. It's not a Pack thing—they cater to the entire community. If you drop in there, tell them I sent you."

"I will," I said, finding myself at least tentatively interested in meeting a female Alpha who could teach me how to fight. I just had to hope she wasn't the type to look down her nose at a weak wolf. "Okay, last question." I gestured to the view from the back windows, through which the Pack forest practically gleamed under the midmorning sun. My wolf was drawn to it—a new sensation that had been creeping up on me the longer I stood here—so I needed to go check it out. "Can anyone just go out there and... shift? And run?"

He chuckled, amused by my naivety, no doubt. "Yes, of course. Leave your purse up here and head on out. The Pack's territory is very expansive, so you can let your girl run until she's had her fill."

I dropped my purse on his desk and hustled my way toward the back doors, the urge to run consuming me in a way that it never had before. "Thank you, Asher!" I called over my shoulder.

He just smiled and waved as I disappeared out into the manicured backyard of the clubhouse and headed straight for the towering thicket of pines that loomed just beyond the gates.

FROM CHAPTER EIGHT

KADY

To no one's surprise—especially mine—my car was the shittiest one in the faculty parking lot at Blackstone Academy. But as it turned out, the teachers' cars were downright boring compared to the flashy luxury vehicles that were parked in the student lot.

I climbed out of the Camry, straightening my fitted white Blackstone Soccer T-shirt and dusting off my black school-issued jogger pants while I took in the tall pines, manicured grass, and the large, stately buildings that made up the campus.

It wasn't my first time here—I'd stopped by yesterday for a meeting with my faculty advisor and fellow Pack member, Helen Hespell, who'd given me a tour of the grounds, shown me to my office in the state-of-the-art gymnasium, and handed me the school handbook and my fall semester schedule before leaving me to explore. I'd spent the afternoon in my office planning my gym classes for the next month and working out which hellish fitness tests I wanted to run my soccer girls through during the first week of tryouts.

It had been blissfully quiet on campus yesterday, but now I was feeling the first-day jitters like I was the new kid in school as I traversed the grounds toward the gym—conveniently located on the exact opposite side of campus.

I walked past the cafeteria—a striking modern building with a sloping metal roof and floor-to-ceiling windows that revealed a large, spacious dining hall. Then off to my right at the front of the grounds was the main academic building—a quintessential historic redbrick schoolhouse covered with creeping ivy that just reached to the top of the four floors. Set directly behind the main building and to my left as I ambled through the massive courtyard was a two-story gothic library, the exterior decorated with high stained glass windows that I knew from the brochure pictures overlooked an atrium-like study area with long tables, old-school green lamps, and rows of bookshelves lining the walls.

I made my way to the east side of campus, which held not only the gym but an entire athletic complex, complete with soccer fields, tennis courts, a brand-new natatorium, and, apparently, a nine-hole golf course. Throngs of students were unhurriedly making their way into the various buildings, dressed in their maroon academy blazers and khaki pants or skirts—the whole picture just reeking of money and privilege.

Even without my nose working at full shifter capacity, it wasn't hard to spot the wolves among the students. That was especially true for the boys since they all looked five years older than the rest of their peers and were tall, well-muscled, and obnoxiously attractive.

Probably cocky little shits, too, if their Alpha is anything to go by.

I'd just reached the gym, pausing near the entrance to return a text to my mom, who'd just sent me a picture of

Sam smiling at the camera and gripping his oversized Moana backpack while he posed in front of his new school, when the sudden scent of wolf invaded my nostrils.

I quickly tapped a heart emoji response to the picture and whirled to face the approaching male—a student, judging by the blazer, black backpack slung lazily over one shoulder, and the obvious and enthusiastic manner in which he was checking me out here in broad daylight at eight o'clock in the morning.

"Hey there," he drawled, his bright green shifter eyes dropping to my chest before darting back to my face. "They didn't tell us we were getting a new Pack girl this year. You a junior or a senior?"

I gave him a blank stare. He wasn't crowding me or invading my personal space, so I was mostly just annoyed that he'd startled me out of my focus on my phone.

"I'm Liam, and I'd be happy to show you around," he went on, inching just a tiny bit closer. "And I like this whole 'fuck you' to the Academy you've got going on by just showing up in your gym clothes too. The rebel thing is a turn on, for sure."

"Sanders! Move along," a deep voice snapped from behind me.

"Yes, go on, please, Liam," a gentler voice chimed in. "You'll see more of *Coach Calloway* in shifter gym."

Liam's eyes went wide before he gave me a sheepish look. "Oh. Shit. Uh, sorry, Coach."

"Uh-huh," I said, crossing my arms over my chest and trying on my best serious teacher face. "It was a nice try, but I'm certain there are plenty of available Pack ladies your own age walking these halls. I suggest you endeavor to keep your eyes on their faces when you speak to them."

Asher appeared at my side, looking amused. The guy

with him stepped up to my other side and gave Liam one more stern glare. "Your ass better be in the pool in five minutes, Sanders. Move it."

"Yes, Coach," he grumbled before slinking away and heading around the side of the gym toward the natatorium.

"Kady, Kady," Asher hummed, tossing an arm over my shoulder. "Breaking hearts already and first period hasn't even started."

"You didn't tell me she was this hot, Ash," the other guy grumbled, sounding irritated, so I didn't think it was exactly meant to be a compliment. "We are going to be batting these hornballs away from her all fucking year."

"Don't whine, Deke," Asher replied. "You get bored and cranky if you aren't busting heads, so I'm just glad you'll have something to keep you occupied."

I eyed Asher's companion. He was human, and he was a few inches taller than Asher, who was probably just under six feet. His dark hair was cropped short, and his broad chest nicely filled out his Blackstone Swimming T-shirt. I spied a sleeve of colorful tattoos wrapped around his right bicep, and he wore a scowl that did nothing to detract from his handsome, masculine face.

"Kady, this is my husband, Deacon," Asher said, giving him a fond smile. "You'll remember we both coach the swim teams here."

I held out my hand to Deacon, who took it in his firm grip. "Kady Calloway. Women's soccer coach, gym teacher, and half-wolf oddball."

The corner of his lips quirked in an almost smile. "I heard. Personally, I don't think this school needs any more supersecret wolf teachers, but it sounds like you may have more in common with me than you do with any of them, so I'll allow it this time."

"Very true." I laughed as we all turned to head through the gym toward our offices. Asher gushed some more about how excited he was that we were going to be teaching together while Deacon generally just grunted or offered one-word answers to my questions. He clearly played the hard-ass, but I was onto him—his perma-scowl couldn't hide the deep devotion shining in his eyes for his husband every time he glanced his way.

The grumpy one is soft for the sunshine one! Swoon.

Asher and Deacon introduced me to a few others on the coaching staff who were lingering in the gym hallway where all of our offices lay, then they dropped me at my own office before disappearing to coach their first-period swim practice.

My first and last periods of the day were office hours, with two gym classes before lunch—first regular gym, then shifter gym—then lunch, one more gym class, and then I would be a teacher's assistant for Helen in a class she was teaching to junior shifter students called Responsible Shifting. Apparently the powers that be within the Pack thought the formerly packless half wolf could benefit from some rudimentary shifter education, and since I'd really needed this job, I hadn't argued.

I glided easily through the motions of my first two gym classes, handing out syllabi and issuing gym clothes while forty students pretended they were listening to me instead of scrolling through their phones. I allowed it for today, but they were going to be sorry tomorrow when we ran a mile for time.

The students in the third-period shifter-only gym class mostly gave me curious looks or ignored me, but there were a group or two of what I easily identified as the popular cliques of wolf kids that snickered as they whispered behind their hands, looks of pity or derision aimed squarely at me while I spoke. I assumed someone had a parent within Pack leadership who squealed about my human parentage and my omega status, but I'd decided before I ever stepped foot in this town that I was going to do my best to ignore that kind of thing.

In this gym, I was the Alpha, and they were going to be running lines until they puked if they decided to be disrespectful. According to Helen, the Dean of the Academy was an unflappable elderly human woman with no idea that a pack of wolves had overrun her school, so if anyone wanted to act up in my class, they could go explain themselves to her.

Asher and Deacon collected me at the fourth-period lunch bell, emerging from the gym's administrative wing after their own office hours, and the three of us marched back across the lush green courtyard toward the cafeteria. We were all wearing our matching coaching outfits, and the blazing September sun warmed me enough to work up a small trickle of boob sweat under my sports bra.

I did not appreciate it.

"How was your morning so far?" Asher asked brightly while Deacon continued to give death stares to every male student he caught staring at my tits. He seemed hilariously oblivious to the multitudes of students checking him out just as blatantly. "They're all usually on good behavior, at least for the first day."

"It was fine," I replied. "The shifter kids are always going to be curious about a new Pack teacher, but it doesn't look like too many of them are aware of what I am, yet." I sighed, reminding myself that I had prepared for this. "But I don't expect that to last."

Asher gave me a sympathetic look. "You're right. It

won't. One thing you should know about all packs, even those as large as this one, is that they are a gossip mill. And while a new omega member is not *that* gossip-worthy, one who is half human definitely is."

"There was some trash talk when Asher married me," Deacon added. "Plenty of them don't care, but there are always the purists who think mating a human is beneath a shifter, or a danger to the survival of the species, or whatever."

"Yes, but that also didn't last," Asher said, chuckling in a way that sounded a little forced. "I'm not particularly powerful or important in the Pack hierarchy, so no one really cared that much who I mated."

I swallowed, an unwanted surge of disappointment punching me in the gut before I pushed it away, choosing instead to give Asher a little teasing smile. "I'm betting they were all just jealous that you locked down such a sexy mate."

He beamed. "For sure," he said, giving me a wink while Deacon tossed a muscled arm over Asher's shoulder and pressed a quick kiss to his temple. I didn't miss the grateful little smile Deacon threw my way before he turned away.

We entered the cafeteria, and I took a moment to gape at the interior. Small food counters dotted the walls, serving what looked like fresh, restaurant-quality meals. There was even a smoothie bar and a fancy coffee cart. The round student tables came complete with chairs made from real wood instead of the plastic ones I recalled from my own high-school days, and there were honest-to-God white freaking tablecloths on each one of them.

"The faculty and staff tables are back here," Asher said, guiding me to the back corner of the room near the tall windows.

FROM CHAPTER EIGHT

The two dedicated staff tables were long and rectangular, sitting side by side and forcing a communal dining experience that I probably would not have been very excited about had I not been adopted by Asher and Deacon. I slid into a chair at the far end of one of the tables, and Asher plopped down next to me. Deacon appeared a few moments later with a stack of what looked like salads in plastic containers, and he handed one to both Asher and me before he sat down next to Asher.

I waved to Helen as she arrived and pulled up a chair across the way with a couple of other older shifter faculty. Asher nodded to them as well and introduced me, pointing out each person's role in the Academy as he went along. A few other coaches I'd already met also joined us.

"This side of this particular table tends to be the Pack faculty area," Asher explained. "Not that we don't mingle with our human counterparts, but we often just congregate together, as is natural for a pack."

Deacon grunted. "Yeah, pretty much everyone's here except—" He trailed off as a pretty young blonde woman about my age sauntered up to the table, the loud clicking of her pointy heels on the tile floor of the cafeteria announcing her arrival. "—Daphne," Deacon finished, sounding less than thrilled.

"Good morning, everyone," she cooed as she pulled a chair up next to Helen and across from Asher. It amazed me she could even sit down in the tight white pencil skirt she had plastered over her frilly magenta sleeveless blouse. "How's the first day been so far? I've already had Margaret Bowman's daughter in my office trying to sweet-talk her way into a schedule change. Bold of her, but *obviously* we only allow students from Alpha and beta lines in the Junior Pack Leaders course." She rolled her eyes and shook her head with a little smile, like we'd all find this as amusing as she clearly did.

"Why would that be obvious?" I asked lightly before popping a piece of chicken into my mouth. "Surely any student with interest in leadership could benefit from such a course."

Daphne's smile faltered, and she glanced at me in confusion, like she'd only just noticed I was here. "I'm sorry —who are you?"

"Daphne, this is Kady Calloway," Asher said cheerfully. "She just joined the Pack over the summer, and she's our new soccer coach. Kady, this is Daphne Murphy. She's in her second year here at the Academy as one of our guidance counselors."

"Oh goodness," Daphne's eyes went wide, then she gave me a knowing look filled with faux sympathy. "I understand now. It may sometimes seem unfair to the wolves at the *lower rungs* of the Pack's order that there aren't leadership opportunities for them, but *of course* a Pack must be led by the strongest wolves for its safety and for order." She quirked her head to the side, continuing to give me a curious stare. "What odd things they must have been teaching you in your previous pack. Or wait—you didn't have a pack. Isn't that right?"

Helen cleared her throat. "Kady, Daphne's mother is a top beta in our Pack and sits on the Alpha's Small Council."

Ah, of course. It figured only a stuck-up elite Pack asshole could dismiss the potential of a "regular" shifter kid so easily. I supposed I'd known that this was how it was going to be around here, but my experiences with Monica's family, Mave, and even Knox hadn't really prepared me. It was a bit of a shock to the system to see firsthand how Pack hierarchy really operated and how it would color my everyday life.

And of course, beta blue-blood Daphne was clearly in the know on what I was, and she had some *assumptions* about me.

"Oh, gosh," I said, shaking my head. "Silly me. As you pointed out, Daphne, I was raised totally in the human world, where I got a degree in education and taught students in, like, regular high schools. We were just always told to encourage curiosity and interest in leadership with *any* student, since you just never really knew who might have a knack for it. I hadn't realized this Pack hadn't progressed into the more *modern* school of thought that is so widely accepted by scholars of education. I clearly *do* have a lot to learn about being wolf."

Deacon snorted into his glass, and I thought I caught a small smile on Helen's face. Asher let out a nervous laugh and squeezed my thigh under the table.

"Yes," Daphne sneered at me. "It sounds like you do have a lot to learn. Starting with a healthy respect for our Pack and its norms and traditions."

"You'll just have to excuse my ignorance, Daphne," I said, putting on my best apologetic face and shrugging a shoulder. "I'm very new. I'll try to remember that any particularly bright or talented Pack student I meet will need to prove their bloodline bona fides before I encourage them to aspire to anything."

"Yes, that is probably wise of you," she said like she was calling my bluff, the color rising in her perfectly contoured cheeks. "I'm *so* glad Helen has you in her class this semester. You'll catch up in no time, sweetie—don't you worry."

She turned then to speak to Helen and another of the

older faculty, dismissing me, and I went back to my salad. I was both disappointed and unsurprised that I'd finally met the kind of person I'd expected a powerful top Pack girl to be.

"I think I'm going to call you Shady Kady from now on," Asher whispered in my ear. "I don't think I've ever seen Daphne rattled. That was bold and impressive, but not exactly good for... blending in."

I sighed. He was probably right, but fingers crossed I could keep my interactions with Daphne and her kind to a minimum.

FROM CHAPTER NINE

KNOX

"Well, if it isn't Knox Monroe himself," Lukas Hendrix said jovially as I entered the staff hallway at the back of the Blackstone Academy gymnasium. I'd finished up my usual daily Pack duties with plenty of time to get an office hour in before I had to start my first men's soccer practice, and I was looking forward to settling in amongst the coaching staff for *no special reason whatsoever*.

I gave Lukas a big smile accompanied by a fist bump and a bro-hug before he continued, "You're kind of a lifesaver, man. Trust Ryan to fall in love and run off to another town at the last goddamn minute, leaving the soccer team without a coach."

"Happy to fill in," I replied. "I've missed the game, and it's kinda fun being back here again."

Lukas was an old classmate of mine from my days at the Academy who had a successful career in playing collegiate basketball before returning here to coach. He was a human, and as far as he knew, I'd taken over my father's business empire and was now just a successful rich guy with a spot on the Academy's Board of Trustees.

FROM CHAPTER NINE

I continued down the hallway toward the office I'd be using while I was here, nodding to a few other faces I recognized. I received a polite, "Good afternoon, Alpha," from Asher Boyd while his human mate just scowled and grunted at me.

"Hey, how's it going, Asher?" I greeted him. "Do you happen to know which office is—"

The distinct scent of what I now knew was hybrid wolf hit my nostrils just as my sensitive ears caught a muttered, "*Nope, nobody's home,*" cutting off any need for me to finish my question. I smirked, catching Asher's curious look at the same time his husband narrowed his eyes at me suspiciously, but I just winked at them and sauntered right on into my little wolf's office without knocking.

Kady did not look at all surprised by my appearance, choosing to lean back in her office chair and cross her arms over her chest (which had the unfortunate effect of obscuring my view of her stellar rack) before giving me an exasperated look. Her dark-brown hair was in the same messy bun on the top of her head that she wore on the first night we met, and her big blue eyes shone with a kind of defiance that made my dick twitch.

"Hey, baby girl," I said with a smooth purr as I helped myself to one of the chairs in front of her desk. "How was your first day of school?"

"One," she said, holding up a finger, "don't call me that while we're at work."

I smirked. "Noted. Will save for our private time together."

"*Two,*" she said, raising her voice and pretending not to have heard my last statement, "I believe your office is down the hall. There is not enough room in here for the two of us *and* your ego."

"You wound me, Little Wolf," I said, clutching my chest with a laugh. "I promise, no one will think anything of me stopping by to check on my newest Pack member and fellow coach. Let me hang out with you for a few minutes. Plus...." I held her big blue eyes with mine, attempting to convey at least a kernel of sincerity. "I missed you."

Her faced softened a bit while the slightest blush bloomed in her cheeks, both of which I had only a second to enjoy before we were interrupted.

"Kady, is this guy bothering you?" Asher's husband said gruffly, appearing in the doorway.

"*Deacon*," I heard Asher hiss from somewhere out in the hallway.

It was Kady's turn to smirk at me. "Yes, but it's okay," she replied, keeping her eyes on mine, and I saw they were now dancing with amusement. "I can handle his bullshit."

"*Kady*," Asher hissed again with urgency, his head popping up over Deacon's shoulder. "Knox is our *Alpha*. I'm sure he's just paying you a polite visit."

I grinned. "Exactly. See? I'm just being a good Alpha to my little wolf."

Deacon snorted from behind me. "And I'm the Queen of fucking England. I knew we were going to have our work cut out for us keeping these hormonal teenagers off of Kady, Ash, but now we have to add your Alpha to the list."

"Deacon!" Asher was entering a mild panic, poor guy.

I decided to cut him a break, rising from my chair and giving Kady one last smile before turning toward them.

"Boys, I'll be heading to my office now, but I appreciate you watching over Kady for me," I said to them both as I reached the doorway. Asher let out a sigh of relief and relaxed a bit, but his husband just continued to scowl at me. I went on, "You can let those horny bastards know—especially my Pack kids—that I will personally destroy any one of them if they so much as glance at Kady's ass."

"Absolutely not, you freaking caveman!" Kady hollered from behind me. "Deacon, ignore him, please."

Asher gaped at us, looking between Kady and me in confusion, while Deacon pinned me with a serious glare. "This is just fucking perfect. I've got my eye on you, dude. You're not my Alpha, and Kady's not used to this Pack shit. Don't take advantage of her."

I lost my air of good humor pretty quickly at that. I didn't blame him for thinking that way, but it was a harsh reminder that my personal history mixed with the extreme power imbalance between Kady and me would have pretty much anyone jumping to the same conclusion, and it hit me like a slap to the face.

I needed to be more careful.

"Hey," I said seriously, looking between Asher and Deacon, and then back at Kady where she still sat, listening intently. "That's not what this is. Kady and I actually have a little bit of personal history, and I'm trusting you both with that information because you seem like you're serious about being good friends to her. I'll let her fill in the details if she wants to. I do know how this looks, but I can assure you that my intentions toward her are one hundred percent genuine."

Asher went all moony eyed at that, giving Kady an excited little smile over my shoulder. Even Deacon softened up just the slightest bit, and I took that as my cue to move along.

"I'll see you guys tomorrow," I said to them as I stepped into the hall. I paused to look back at Kady, who had an unreadable expression on her face. "And I'll see you down at the fields, Little Wolf."

FROM CHAPTER NINE

Made in the USA
Columbia, SC
03 November 2024